M000222441

DRAGON'S TEARS

THE DRAGON SHIFTER'S MATES #2

EVA CHASE

INK SPARK PRESS

Dragon's Tears

Book 2 in the Dragon Shifter's Mates series

All rights reserved. This book or any portion thereof may not be reproduced or used in any manner without the express written permission of the author, except for the use of brief quotations in a book review.

This is a work of fiction. Any resemblance to actual persons, living or dead, or actual events is purely coincidental.

First Digital Edition, 2017

Copyright © 2017 Eva Chase

Cover design: Another World Designs

Ebook ISBN: 978-0-9959865-6-5

Paperback ISBN: 978-0-9959865-7-2

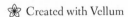 Created with Vellum

CHAPTER 1

Ren

IF SOMEONE HAD TOLD me a week ago that soon I'd be shopping for camping gear with the four hottest guys in existence, I'd have called up the loony bin to collect them. But there I was, in a little shop in a town I'd never heard of until two days ago, doing my best not to melt as one of those gorgeous guys helped me into a down-filled jacket. His fingers skimmed my chest, sending a pleasant shiver over my skin.

It wasn't just Aaron's touch that had me on the verge of puddle-dom. The late June sun was shining brightly through the shop's windows, and the still air between the racks of outdoor clothes, backpacks, and other gear was thick with warmth. I squirmed inside the jacket.

"Are you sure I need to be *this* suited up?"

Aaron smiled at me with a mischievous glint in his bright blue eyes. Between those baby-blues and his

1

golden-blond hair, he could have passed for a Disney prince. Although I wasn't sure I'd ever seen a Disney hero quite that buff. I'd definitely never seen one who could make me tingle between my legs with just a glance.

"You said you're not sure how far into the mountains we'll need to go," he said, with the faint rasp that gave a little flavor to his even voice. "It'll be a lot colder at the higher altitudes."

"And we wouldn't want our Princess of Flames getting frozen," Marco drawled, leaning against a rack with his usual crooked grin. It fit the rakish playboy vibe he already had going on with his spiky black hair, the little scar through his arched eyebrow, and his refusal to take any situation completely seriously. His indigo gaze swept over my body, sending a fresh wave of heat through me. His grin widened. "As sad as I am to see you covered up, of course."

I glowered at him as I shrugged the jacket off. "I'm sure you'll survive without a view of my cleavage for a few days."

Marco chuckled. "I do have the rest of my life to appreciate it after that."

Oh, yeah. That was the detail I'd have found hardest to swallow before *my* life turned upside down about a week ago. The four guys doing their shopping with me were all shifters—and not any old shifters, but the alphas of their respective kin-groups. Marco could turn into a sleek black jaguar. He ruled over the feline kin. As leader of the avian shifters, Aaron's animal side was an impressive golden eagle.

And me? I'd discovered I was a dragon shifter. One of

only two left in the world, if my mother was still alive. If she wasn't, then I was the very last. And my job was to unite shifter kind by taking all four alphas as my mates. No pressure or anything.

There were worse things than being expected to hook up with four completely smokin' guys, don't get me wrong. But for a girl who'd never gotten past second base in the first twenty-one years of her life—and who'd had no idea shifters even existed—all that attention could feel a little overwhelming.

I slung the jacket over my arm. "It fits and it's comfortable. And I want to get going. I'll take this one."

It had been seven years since my mother had passed through Sunridge, Wyoming and left her message for me with an enchantment on the town monument, but I didn't want to wait a second longer than I had to before I found out what had happened to her after.

Nate ambled over, a couple of rolled sleeping bags tucked under his brawny arms. His bear side came through in his tall, well-built body and his chestnut brown hair. But his expression when he looked at me was all gentle warmth. He might be a grizzly when we were under attack, but with me he was a total teddy bear.

"Do you figure we'll be up there over at least one night, Ren?" he said. His rich baritone voice never failed to warm me up too.

"I'm... not really sure," I admitted. We'd ended up here in Sunridge after following a trail of clues my mother had left me. When I'd touched the obelisk in the town square, I'd gotten a vision of her telling me there was something I needed to find up one particular

3

mountain. Some kind of power she'd gone to retrieve seven years ago.

She'd never come back. I'd spent all those years with no idea where she'd gone or what had become of her. Really, getting some answers about that mattered more to me than any special powers. I could transform into a dragon—a big, fast, fire-breathing dragon. Wasn't that enough?

The thought sent an anxious tremor up my arm. Before I'd quite realized what I was doing, my hand had snatched a metal karabiner out of a basket and tucked it into my sleeve. Damned pickpocket instincts. They always kicked in when I was nervous. I pulled it out and set it back in the basket with a flush of embarrassment, but thankfully none of the guys commented on my slip.

"It'll be better for us to bring more supplies than we need than not enough," Aaron said to Nate. He was the most practical of my guys, which I appreciated a heck of a lot when I had so much still to learn about shifter abilities —and limitations. "Sleeping bags will be a lot more comfortable than just the blankets we've got in the SUV." He turned, looking toward the fourth member of my alpha squad. "Didn't you say there's a tent in the trunk, West?"

The wolf shifter nodded where he was lurking near the shop's front door. The sunlight streaming in caught on the silver strands mixed with his light auburn hair. Like his animal, he was all lean muscle, on display now with his arms crossed over his firm chest.

West was frowning, but that didn't mean much. He frowned at pretty much everything, especially if it had anything to do with me. He'd made it very clear that he wasn't on board with this whole "destined to mate with the dragon shifter" idea just yet. I guessed I couldn't exactly blame him, considering the chaos that shifter tradition had apparently thrown the kin-groups into when my mother had disappeared from the community with me sixteen years ago.

I wouldn't have minded him remembering that *I'd* had nothing to do with the decision to leave before he turned his gruffness on me, though.

"I'm not sure the tent we have is big enough for the five of us, but with the trouble we've had getting here, we'll probably want a couple of us on watch at any given time anyway," West said. "There's nothing to carry it with, though. We'll need to grab some packs. I'm assuming we're not going to be able to drive right up to this dragon shifter treasure." His dark green eyes slid to me with that last sentence.

"I don't know," I said. "This trek wasn't *my* idea. Believe me, I wish my mother had given us more detailed instructions too."

"We're all following you in this, Sparks," he muttered. "Keep that in mind."

"I think it's a safe assumption that we'll have to go part of the way on foot," Aaron broke in, calmly. His practical side made him a good peacemaker too. "And we'll want to pick up food for the trip, since we can't be sure of the hunting."

"I saw a decent-sized grocery store on our way into town," Nate said.

"Perfect." I carried my jacket over to the counter. "I

hope you all have good credit." Especially since I didn't even own a credit card. I'd only just gotten off the streets a couple months ago.

Marco chuckled. "Don't worry, princess. Money is not an object for any of us."

He paid for our new gear, which thankfully Sunridge had in large supply, being so close to prime hiking and camping ground. Then we drove over to the grocery store. I stayed in my seat as the guys started to clamber out.

"Grab me some spicy beef jerky and Doritos if they have them," I said. "Otherwise I trust your judgment. I want to give Kylie a heads up before we're potentially out of cell tower range."

Nate's head snapped around. "You shouldn't hang back alone. I'll stay in the car with you."

I was tempted to tell him I'd be fine, but the fact was I might not be. We'd already been attacked by a group of rogue shifters on our way into town—presumably the same group that had killed my fathers and my sisters all those years ago. That was what had sent my mother on the run with me. You couldn't really blame her, considering the circumstances.

I'd managed to complete my shift into a dragon for the first time to fend off today's attack, and I'd totally fried their apparent leader, but a few of them had gotten away. And we didn't know for sure how many others there might be around.

The rogues didn't play by shifter rules. They were willing to use weapons on their own kind, even guns, which the alphas had told me was strictly forbidden.

Shifters healed quickly, but the sealed wound on my arm where I'd caught a bullet still ached.

So I smiled at Nate and said, "Sure. Just don't be offended if I'm giving all my attention to my phone."

Nate reached over the back of the seat to squeeze my shoulder. "I wouldn't get in the way of you talking to your friend."

The bear shifter stayed behind me while the other guys headed into the store. I pulled out my phone. *Hey, Ky. How are you feeling?*

My best friend had been with us a couple days ago during the first attempt the rogue shifters had made on my life. They'd nearly killed her. Which was why I'd insisted she head home to Brooklyn once she'd healed up instead of coming along with us.

She texted back almost immediately. *I'm doing good! I'd say 95% at this point.* She added a winking emoji. *Should be 100% by tomorrow. What have you been up to? Did you make it to Sunridge? What did you find there? I need answers!!!*

I had to smile. Kylie's hyper energy came through clearly even in text form. I could picture her so easily, lounging on one of the porch chairs in the shifter village where she'd been recovering, grinning as bright as her neon pink pixie cut.

As I tried to decide what to say, my smile faded. I didn't really want to worry my bestie by telling her about the second attack, especially when she was too far away to do anything. She'd already come running to my rescue once. Right now she needed to focus on making sure *she* stayed okay. But there was one thing I had to share.

I managed a full shift this morning. You're talking to a bona fide dragon now!

Holy shit! That's amazing, Ren. I so cannot wait for you to demonstrate for me.

First thing when I get back. But we might be gone for a while longer. My mom left another message for me here. There's this stone with a picture on it that seems to be tied to the dragon shifters somehow... Another trail for us to follow.

Any sign of your mom herself? Kylie asked.

I bit my lip. *No. It doesn't really look good. The way she talked in the message she left... It sounded like someone was after her. And that she planned on coming back to me if she could. So since she didn't...*

I'm so sorry, Ren. But maybe it's not as bad as it looks.

I wanted to think that, so badly. That Mom was imprisoned or forced into deeper hiding or something else that had stopped her from returning to New York City—something other than her being dead. But the farther we came without finding any recent trace of her presence, the harder it got.

I'll keep hoping until I know for sure, I wrote. *But anyway, we might be out of service range for a few days. So don't worry if you don't hear from me! Just keep looking after yourself.*

I'm on it. You take care of you too. Although it's hard to be too worried when I know you've got those four hunks of manliness chomping to defend you. And get it on with you. Any progress in that area? Devil emoji.

I rolled my eyes, but my cheeks had flushed at the same time. There had been, actually. I'd taken my first major step toward claiming my destiny as leader of the shifters last night—by officially claiming Aaron as my mate.

In other words, we'd had sex. Really, really good sex, that still sent a giddy quiver through me when I thought back to it.

But talking about my first time via text just felt wrong. That kind of girl talk, I wanted to have face-to-face with my bestie.

More on that when I get back, I wrote.

Aw, way to leave a girl hanging! I want all the deets the second I see you.

I promise.

There might be a lot more details by the time I got to hang out with Kylie again. To take on my full role as dragon shifter, I was supposed to be getting fully intimate with all four of the guys. And Marco and Nate, at least, had shown plenty of enthusiasm in that area. But just losing my V-card had been a big step. As much as I was drawn toward all of the guys—even West—I wasn't about to jump in the sack with all of them at once just like that.

As appealing as that image suddenly was. Exactly how many guys *could* you get it on with at the same time?

I was feeling a little hotter than I could blame on the sun when the other three alphas returned with their haul. They tossed the grocery bags in the back with the rest of the gear and piled in. I'd taken the front passenger spot since I was the one with the best idea where we were going—as shaky as even that was. Aaron, who'd spent the most time eyeballing the maps, took the wheel.

"The road goes about a quarter of the way up the

mountain before taking a sideways route around it," he said. "Let me know if you sense anything along the way that tells us which direction we should take, or where we should stop."

I nodded. All thoughts of bedroom-type activities faded into the back of my mind behind a jittering of anticipation. I didn't know what was waiting for us in the mountains, but based on the way Mom had talked in the vision she'd left for me, I was sure this was the end of the path. I'd have my answers soon.

Aaron turned the car toward the mountain with the dual peaks, the one that matched the carving on the obelisk. The carving had shown a flame between those peaks as well. I guessed that was how the sun must look as it rose and flared between them. And maybe the image hinted at the power Mom had said was hidden there.

"You've done all that reading into shifter history," I said to Aaron. "Do you have any idea what kind of 'power' my mother could have been talking about?"

He shook his head. "The dragon shifters have always kept some things to themselves. It's such a close bond, from mother to daughters over the centuries, just that one line that all of shifter-kind revolves around. It makes sense that they'd have their secrets."

Such a close bond. Mom and I had always been close, for sure. We'd only had each other the nine years we'd lived in hiding together in New York City.

But we hadn't bonded over our dragon shifter natures. She'd locked all my memories of that part of our lives away, along with my powers. They were only just starting to trickle back in. I had to assume she'd only been trying to protect me, but now that I needed my powers, I couldn't help wishing she'd found another way.

A nagging sensation crept over my skin as the road rose to follow the slope of the mountain. It was more than anticipation now. A faint pull tugged me toward the slope, urging me upward. As if I were being called by someone who knew me and wanted to welcome me back.

"Dragon shifters do seem to have excellent taste in dramatic scenery," Marco remarked behind me. The high mountain range that surrounded Sunridge spilled out all around us, starkly majestic.

The road wove back and forth as it climbed the mountain, and then veered sharply to the left. We'd only driven a few seconds longer when the faint pull I'd felt turned into a pinching tug.

"Stop," I said. Aaron glanced over at me and hit the brake.

"Did you see something?" he said

"Not yet, but there's something here. I can *feel* it."

He pulled onto the shoulder a short distance along the road, where a low fence surrounded an overlook. I hopped out of the SUV the second it had stopped moving. My sneakers thudded against the pavement as I hurried across the road. I followed the steep rock face on the other side back to the sharp left we'd taken.

Here. The pull urged me upward. I gripped the uneven surface of the rock and hauled myself up the steep slope. I might not have full command of my shifting abilities yet, but I'd had a shifter's strength and agility with me my entire life.

After what would be a quick scramble up the rock

face, the slope evened out. A shallow hollow ran through the stone, slanting slightly upward. The second my gaze rested on that hollow, the nagging sensation crept deeper, into my lungs.

That was our path. I knew it down to my bones.

My alphas had gathered at the edge of the road beneath me. I jumped back down. The exhilaration of the leap wasn't quite as thrilling now that I'd experienced actual flight. Damn, I couldn't wait to get back into dragon form. It was too bad I'd only been able to hold it for a few minutes that first time. I'd have to work on my endurance.

"We need to go that way," I said, pointing. "Farther up the mountain."

West eyed the slope and grimaced. "Good thing we're only bringing the one tent."

Marco gave him a light punch to the shoulder. "Quit grumbling and help me pack up, wolf boy."

My heart sank a bit as they sauntered back to the SUV. All four of them were following this path for me, because I said it was important. But I really didn't have a clue what was waiting for us up there.

"I don't know how far we'll have to go," I said. "It could be a long trek."

"We're prepared for that," Aaron said with a reassuring smile. "Your mother led us here for a reason."

Nate squeezed my shoulder. "We all believe in you, Ren. Even West, no matter how grouchy he's being about it. Your instincts won't lead us wrong."

I turned toward the tallest of my alphas, drawn to the solid heat of his body. Nate seemed to know exactly what

I needed. He wrapped his brawny arms around me in a hug, ducking his head next to mine.

The brush of his cheek against my temple set a flare of a completely different kind of need through me. I eased back just enough to raise my head and bring my lips to his.

Nate leaned into the kiss, returning it firmly but tenderly. The heat of him washed right through my entire body. Oh, yes, a very large part of me was looking forward to getting *completely* acquainted with all of my guys.

But now was obviously not the time for that. I kissed him one more time, hard enough that he rumbled with pleasure deep in his chest, and then I made myself step back. My cheeks were flushed, but I suddenly felt twice as steady.

"Let's get our gear and get going."

CHAPTER 2

Ren

SEVERAL HOURS UP THE TRAIL, I was starting to wonder if we'd really needed to bring quite so much stuff. I could survive without a sleeping bag, right? Who needed changes of clothes? What good was food? I *knew* the guys had given me the lightest pack, and it still felt like there was a ton of bricks weighing on my shoulders.

Apparently I needed to work on that endurance thing in more than just the shifting department. I hadn't had the opportunity to get a whole lot of practice mountain-trekking in NYC.

I didn't want to look like a wimp when my alphas were striding along like the effort was nothing, so I gritted my teeth and kept walking. But I couldn't say I was upset when Aaron paused and touched one of the walls of rock that had gradually been rising on either side of us. They loomed over the path now, not so high they blocked out the sinking sun, but enough that there was no hope of taking a shortcut out.

"There've been fae up here," Aaron said.

"What?" West pushed past Nate to stride over. Aaron pointed to a mark in the smooth rock—a couple of intersecting lines with a glow so faint I wouldn't have noticed it if he hadn't drawn my attention. West's shoulders tensed. The rest of us drew closer.

"It looks old," Marco said. "They haven't charged that any time recently."

"Charged?" I repeated.

"With magic." He waved his hand toward the lines. "The fae are big fans of making things shiny."

"So by fae, we're talking... fairies, right?" I guessed if shifters and vampires were real, there was no reason Tinkerbell shouldn't be too.

West cut his gaze toward me. "Just like we're a far cry from werewolves, the fae aren't anything like your fairy tales. They're nothing you want to mess with."

"They've had kind of a chip on their shoulder since human beings started taking over so much of their territory," Marco elaborated. "They do love their privacy."

"But mountains aren't exactly their usual type of wilderness. They usually prefer places where things *grow*." Aaron studied the path ahead with a thoughtful expression.

Nate set his hands on my shoulders. "We've got to keep going either way. The sooner we find what we're looking for, the sooner we can leave and not have to worry about dealing with the fae at all."

No one could argue with that. We started tramping along again, but we were all eyeing the stone walls a lot more carefully now. The path was maybe seven feet wide, not a whole lot of room to maneuver if we had to fight. Which West, at least, seemed to think was a possibility. But Marco had said it was humans the fae took issue with.

"How do the fae feel about shifters?" I asked.

West made a sound somewhere between a grunt and a wordless muttering, as if he thought the question was ridiculous. Aaron ignored him. "We used to have decent relations with them," he said. "Our interests and needs are pretty different, but we share an appreciation for wild, open spaces and privacy from humans. Unfortunately we've had some... clashes in the last several decades."

"As humans expand their cities and towns, we end up having to move around too," Nate put in. "And the fae are getting more protective of their territory. I've heard they used to be okay with us sharing ground when we needed to shift and let off some steam."

"And now they're as likely to try to barbeque us," Marco said. "But those tensions might get better once you're established in your role, princess. It's harder to maintain good relations when we're a little fractured even amongst ourselves."

Had Mom ever talked about that, when I'd been little? I reached back into my fragmented memories, the ones she'd buried with her magic after we'd fled. They hadn't come back easy, and it was still hard to piece anything very coherent together. I slipped my hand into my pocket at the same time, closing my fingers around the locket she'd given me before she left that last time. The one that had drawn my alphas to me. I'd had to stop wearing it around my neck to make sure the chain didn't snap during an unexpected shift.

I could feel a hint of the magic in the warm metal now, whispering against my palm. It helped center my mind on those distant memories.

An image swam up of Mom standing at the edge of a forest, talking with a tall, slender man whose skin was so pale it looked almost blue. He had a faint sheen to him too, that lit up where the sun touched him. I was crouched in the grass, watching, my heart hammering. Both nervous and excited.

"Who *was* that?" I'd asked Mom later.

"One of the fae," she'd said. "I need to negotiate with them from time to time, on behalf of our community. You won't see them very often, though." She'd paused, her expression going distant. "I suppose it's a little sad, how little we interact and how formally. My grandmother told me that long ago the fae and the dragon shifters shared a special connection. But that's faded now."

Then she'd kissed my forehead and ushered me to the dining room for our dinner.

A lump rose in my throat. I hadn't known her properly in the last sixteen years, because she hadn't let me know her. And now that I knew who we were, I might never see her again in anything but a memory or a vision.

A warmth brushed my skin, like the feeling of her presence when we'd sat shoulder to shoulder on our couch. At first I thought it was just because of my reminiscing. Then my gaze fell on a small swath of parallel scratches dug into the rock wall just ahead.

My pulse stuttered. I stopped as I reached them, running my fingers over the narrow crevices. A stronger sense of my mother's presence rippled over me. I could almost smell her, like lilies and honey.

"My mother was definitely here," I said when I could manage to speak. "She must have shifted—she made these marks. I can feel her in them."

"That's pretty dainty work for dragon talons," Marco remarked.

"She probably meant for you to see them," Nate said. "To know that she's with you here, one way or another."

Right. And there was a chance whatever lay ahead would lead me the rest of the way to her. I squared my shoulders under the straps of my pack and strode on.

Aaron made a humming noise. "That doesn't look good."

My head jerked up. "What?"

The question had hardly fallen from my mouth when I saw it. Down the path, a jumble of boulders had tumbled down to fill the gap between the walls. There must have been a rockslide. Just what we needed—more climbing.

But as we hurried closer, I realized our situation was more complicated than that. The highest boulders had fallen at an angle, jutting out over the lower ones. There was no way to climb that heap unless we could turn off gravity. Which as far as I knew was not a skill any shifter was gifted with.

We stopped at the edge of the landslide's shadow and peered up at it. Aaron rubbed his square jaw. Marco stalked from one side of the path to the other, looking very much the jaguar in that moment. Nate moved to test one of the boulders within reach, as if he thought he could dig his way through, and West made a warning noise.

"Don't bring the whole damn pile down on our heads."

"We've got to get past it somehow," Nate said.

"I can fly," Aaron said. "But I wouldn't be able to carry more than my pack in eagle form."

He wasn't the only one who could fly. "I can carry a lot more than that," I said. "Hell, in dragon form I could blast that pile right down so we don't have to deal with it on the way back." The sun was waning, and we hadn't seen another person since we'd left the road. I didn't think any humans would spot my dragon form all the way up here.

Nate frowned. "You only shifted for the first time this morning. You might not have recovered enough energy yet."

I shrugged off my pack and reached for the hem of my shirt. Shifting and clothes didn't get along so well, especially when you shifted into as large a creature as I did. "Can't hurt to try, can it?"

Marco leaned against the rock wall with an amused smile. "I, for one, am going to enjoy watching that."

"Here," Aaron said. He found the padded jacket I'd bought and brought it over as I tugged off my shirt and bra. "You won't be able to concentrate on shifting if you're freezing. Just keep it on your shoulders so it'll fall off when you make the transformation."

"Thanks." I tugged the jacket over me like a cape, thankful for both the warmth and the little bit of modesty. These guys had been stripping down whenever they needed to shift, regardless of who was around, all their lives. It was going to take a little while for me to get used to the casual nudity side of shifter-dom.

I kicked off my pants and undies and knelt down so the jacket hung around most of my body. I'd barely noticed the cooling mountain air on our hike up. It'd been warm when we'd started, and then *I'd* been warm from the hiking. Now the chilly air seeped over my bare skin.

I wouldn't mind it so much when I had scales. How could I bring them out? I'd shifted in the heat of battle before, desperate to protect my alphas before they died protecting *me*. We didn't face a threat anywhere near that urgent right now. How much could I even control that power?

The doubts wriggled through my mind. I closed my eyes and inhaled deeply, trying to will them away. I knew the dragon inside me now. I knew what it felt like to expand into that body, to spread those wings. All I had to do was get back there.

I thought back to the sensation of stretching muscles, of scales forming over my softer skin. But the memory didn't come alone. The *crack* of the gunshots echoed through my mind. Cries of pain. All the awful sounds of the rogue's ambush. My back went rigid.

No, that was no good. I had to let go of that stuff. I *was* a dragon. I had to just *be* one.

"If you can't manage it, we'll find another way," Nate said. "Don't push yourself too hard."

A spark of annoyance lit in my chest. Why shouldn't I push myself? Weren't all of them pushing themselves on my behalf all the time? I wasn't some weakling who needed to be coddled. I was a fucking *dragon*.

That flare of determination shot through my body. Yes, that was what I needed. I held onto it and dove headfirst into the searing sensation racing over my skin. Into it and through and out and up, limbs expanding, neck extending, every part of me stretching free. My head lengthened into jaws lined with sharp teeth, a smoky flavor trickling on my tongue. Fire danced in my lungs.

I launched myself up toward the sky, giddy. The shift pinched at my joints, but I didn't mind that little bit of strain. I'd done it. This was who I was.

The wind buffeted me as I swooped around. I drank in the pleasure of flight for a moment, and then I dipped back down. I didn't know how long I'd be able to hold this form. I couldn't forget the whole reason I'd taken it on right now.

The heap of boulders looked like pebbles to my dragon self. I dropped down over the highest one and grasped it between my hind feet. My talons closed around it and wrenched it off the pile. With a few flaps of my wings, I deposited it away from the path on the mountainside.

One down, a dozen or so more to go.

I tossed another boulder aside, and another, and another. The pinching I'd noticed earlier started to creep through my wings and chest. I'd already held the shift longer than last time. My body was getting worn out. Damn it, I wasn't done yet.

But I'd handled the worst of it. I eyeballed the remaining pile, only half as high as when I'd started. My alphas had backed up to give me room. If I just took a good running start at it...

I flew down the path the way we'd come. As I swung around, a flicker of movement caught my eye. I hesitated, peering down, but I couldn't see anything except shadows in the path below me. It'd probably been the motion of my own shadow I'd seen.

Gathering my strength, I raced toward the heap as fast as my wings could flap. The air whistled past me. My expanded heart thudded with glee. My dragon lips parted in what must have been a dragon-ish grin.

At the last second, I heaved my hind legs down and forward. I crashed into the pile feet first. The impact radiated through my body, but I hopped upright before I could fall on my back. The remaining boulders tumbled down the path with a rattling thunder, spreading out so we'd be able to walk between them.

Not a second too soon. That bone-deep exhaustion was rolling over me again. I sank down on the ground, hunching my back, shrinking into myself. The scales contracted back into my skin. In a moment, all that remained of my dragon form was the taste of smoke in the back of my mouth.

My human body felt tired too, but not enough to dampen my sense of victory. "I did it!" I said, springing up. "There you go, path cleared, dragon shifter at your service." I gave a little bow.

"Nicely done," Aaron said with a chuckle. Marco grinned and clapped his hands in a round of applause. Nate smiled proudly. And West—

West's eyes were fixed on my body, which in my enthusiasm I'd forgotten was now completely uncovered. At my glance, his gaze jerked back to my face. In that first instant as we stared at each other, hunger lingered in his expression, too intense for him to completely rein in. Despite the cool air, a wave of heat washed over me.

He turned with a snap, taking that heat with him.

CHAPTER 3

Aaron

WHEN I DUCKED into the tent, Serenity was sitting cross-legged on her sleeping bag in the middle, grimacing at her phone.

I sank down onto my own sleeping bag at her right. "Is something the matter?"

"Oh, I knew there probably wouldn't be much reception up here, but I was hoping I'd be able to update Kylie at least one more time before we lost it completely." She sighed and tucked the phone into her pack's outer pocket. "I guess I'd run out of charge before too long anyway. No handy electrical sockets up here!"

"We've made good time," I said, sensing the distress under her joke. I'd seen her with her friend enough to know how much they'd relied on each other. Serenity could rely on the four of us, her alphas, now, but of course it'd take time for her to adjust to that. She'd only just found enough trust to welcome me fully as her mate.

That thought drew me closer to her. I leaned in, and an answering spark of attraction lit in her amber eyes. She lifted her head to meet my kiss eagerly.

When I'd first met our dragon shifter, I'd wondered if the unshakeable pull I felt toward her—to be near her, to touch her, to bring her pleasure—would ease off once our mate-bond was consummated. It seemed the answer was no. Since last night, my desire for her hadn't eased off at all. I'd managed to keep my equipment in my pants for twenty-seven years, and now it was agonizing to imagine going even one night without hearing her moaning beneath me.

She made a sound that was almost a moan now as I teased my tongue into her mouth. Her fingers trailed up my neck to tangle in my hair. She tugged me even closer. Sparks of pleasure raced over my scalp. I cupped her jaw, kissing her harder. Then I let my hand slip down over her shirt to caress her breast. The nipple peaked beneath my palm.

A whimper crept from her throat. She arched into my touch encouragingly. Her curves were so soft under my fingers, but I could still feel the strength all through her body. The combination thrilled me. What a woman my mate was.

I edged up the hem of her shirt to touch her skin to skin. Serenity let out a gasp against my mouth when my fingertips grazed the tip of her breast through her bra. Her fingers curled against my shoulders. Then she tensed.

I eased back to see her face. "Are you all right?"

Her mouth twisted. Desire still burned in her eyes. "I want to keep going. But... West is supposed to be sleeping in the tent the first half of the night too, isn't he? He might come in while we're..." She gestured between us with a crooked smile.

Ah. It was going to take time for her to adjust to that aspect of our relationship too. I stroked her cheek and the side of her neck.

"You know if all goes well between the group of us, there'll be moments in the future when the other alphas aren't just seeing you with me... they'll be joining in as well."

She drew her legs up to her chest. "I know. It's still a little hard to wrap my head around. It's not like I've ever tried a *three*some before, let alone a... five-some?"

If Serenity had grown up among the shifters, seeing her mother with her four fathers, she wouldn't feel this hesitation. And that was the fault of the rogues who'd ripped her family apart with their bloodshed.

My jaw clenched for a second before I forced it to relax. The past was gone, as horrific as it had been. All we could do was move forward from there. And make sure none of the rogues who remained got another chance at harming the dragon shifter we still had.

Serenity didn't deserve to be rushed, but it wouldn't be right for me to encourage her to see me as her only mate either. I pressed a gentle kiss to her lips. "We can give you time. Don't feel you have to rush things. And I'm here for you, however you need me. But I think it'll be good for you to try to keep your mind open. Dragon shifters aren't meant for only one mate. I won't be enough to satisfy you on my own."

The glint in her eyes turned mischievous. "You're doing an awfully good job so far." She kissed me again, long and slow. Then she scooted her sleeping bag as close to mine as she could get. "Hold me until I fall asleep?"

I lay down next to her and wrapped my arm around her waist, tipping my face next to hers. "Until then and after, Serenity."

~

Ren

My toe caught on a ridge in the path, and I stumbled forward. A curse fell from my mouth, but I caught my balance before Nate's helping hand reached me. "I'm okay, I'm okay."

"Whoever picked this route obviously wasn't too concerned about ease of travel," Marco said, raising his eyebrows as he took in our surroundings. "A little redecorating might be in order."

I couldn't argue. If I'd thought yesterday's hike had been difficult, today's was downright brutal. The path had veered sharply upward through the morning, and just after we'd stopped for a quick lunch, the walls above slanted together to form a ceiling overhead. We were walking through a cave now. A cave with a really uneven floor and only dim light from the occasional gaps in the ceiling. Our steps echoed faintly through the cavernous passage.

The temperature had dropped at the same time. A damp chill brushed my face as I trudged on. I was very glad for that down jacket now. But the tug inside me kept urging me onward, more insistently now than before. Whatever we were heading toward, we were definitely getting closer.

"Have you gotten any clearer sense of what we're looking for or how far ahead it might be?" Aaron asked me.

I shook my head. "The feeling I have is still just a vague pull. But I know we're going the right way." If that feeling hadn't been enough to confirm it, just an hour ago I'd spotted another score mark where Mom's energy had lingered. She'd entered this cave too, seven or so years ago. Entered it and left her mark for me to find.

We'd also spotted a couple slivers of fae magic etched in the walls, although nothing the guys had thought was recent.

Something split the hazy gray tunnel ahead of us. I squinted at it. After several more steps, I made out what it was—a seam of rock. The cave was splitting into two passages.

"I'm not much of a fan of mazes," West muttered.

Neither was I, but as we reached the branching, the pull inside me tugged to the left clearly enough. "We go that way," I said, pointing. "No problem."

"I trust your instincts," Aaron said, "but I don't like the additional possibilities for an ambush when there are multiple passages to move between. I think we should quickly scout out both sides—check for any signs of potential enemies."

"Fine," West said, stalking toward the passage to the right. "Let's just get on with it."

"Fifteen minutes, and if you haven't seen any reason to worry by then, meet back up," Aaron called after him. He headed down the left passage, leaving me with Marco and Nate.

The big bear shifter crossed his arms over his chest, looming over me as if there were some immediate threat I needed to be defended from. I appreciated that he wanted to look out for me, but sometimes his protectiveness felt a little smothering.

"I'm pretty sure there's nothing around here except for rocks," I said. "Unless there are some rock demons or something you guys haven't bothered to tell me exist, we should be fine."

"No rock demons," Marco said with a grin. "As much as I might enjoy a little break. Hiking, hiking, hiking does get monotonous."

"We've seen those signs that the fae have been through here," Nate said. "It's better to be cautious than to put you at risk."

I couldn't say I exactly minded this kind of break. I set down my pack and rolled my shoulders. They throbbed with the motion.

"Need a little help with those?" Marco said in a suggestive tone.

I rolled my eyes at him, and his grin widened. But I

actually wouldn't mind a little assistance working out the kinks in my muscles. "Give them everything you've got," I said, shrugging my jacket down to give him better access.

Marco's lithe hands settled on my shoulders over the fabric of my shirt. He dug his thumbs into my muscles with the perfect amount of pressure. I groaned at the burn spreading through my shoulders, and he chuckled. Suddenly the cave's air felt a whole lot warmer.

A pattering sound carried from the other end of the cave, back the way we'd come. Nate's back went rigid. He turned toward it, his bulky arms flexing. No other sounds followed, but he didn't relax.

"It's probably nothing," I said. "Just a pebble falling off the ceiling."

"I should take a look to make sure," Nate said. Then he hesitated, his gaze moving to Marco. "You'll watch out for Ren?"

"Of course," Marco said, sounding amused. "Anyway, there's one of the rest of you in any direction an enemy could come at us from. If you start screaming, we'll know to get moving."

Nate glowered at the jaguar shifter and headed down the cave. Marco resumed my shoulder massage. It didn't take long before the bear shifter's brawny form disappeared into the darkness. Marco leaned closer, letting his fingers dip down to my collarbone.

"Finally we're alone," he murmured in my ear.

A shiver of anticipation ran through me even as I smiled. "And what exactly are you assuming will happen now that we are?"

"I make no assumptions. Only offers. How would you like to spend the rest of our wait in a way we'll both enjoy very much?"

"You think so highly of your abilities," I teased. Then his hands dipped right under my bra, tracing the sensitive skin just above the tips of my breasts, and my breath caught. My body moved of its own accord. I leaned back against him, tilting my head as he pressed his mouth to the side of my neck.

"For good reason," Marco said, his breath hot against my skin. It was so hard to resist the passionate need flaring up from my core. And why should I resist it? Like Aaron had said last night, all four of these guys were my mates. I needed to get more comfortable with all of them. To open myself up to the experience.

I turned in Marco's embrace and yanked his mouth to mine. He kissed me, a hungry sound reverberating from his chest. His hands slipped up my back under my shirt and nimbly unhooked my bra. As the cups loosened, he reached for my breasts again, swiveling his thumbs around my nipples and then flicking over them until I gasped.

My hips canted toward his. He dropped one hand to grasp my waist and spun us around so he could lean me against the stone wall. His touch teased over my hips and thighs. I kissed him hard, not caring about the rough surface behind me, just wanting to feel more.

Marco's lips moved away from mine to nibble a tingling line along my jaw. "Oh, my Princess of Flames," he said between nips. "You're amazing. There's no other word for it. I couldn't have imagined a better mate."

I mumbled something inarticulate and encouraging, lost in the haze of pleasure. My eyelids fluttered. The light in the cave behind Marco seemed to flutter with them—and to solidify into a humanoid form.

We weren't alone anymore.

CHAPTER 4

Ren

A YELP BROKE from my throat. I jerked away from Marco and the figure beyond him, smacking the back of my head on the wall of the cave. Marco whirled to place himself between me and the figure in one smooth movement. What must have been an instinctive shout of warning burst out of him, but his shoulders came down when he set eyes on the strange woman. He drew himself up straighter.

"You know, I really thought the fae had better manners," he said.

The fae. Yes, the woman standing at the other side of the passage was as slim and pale as the man I remembered Mom talking to. Her skin, hair, and filmy dress had the same bluish shine, a little dampened here in the dimness of the cave.

I fumbled to fix my bra, my face flushing. This wasn't

exactly how I'd have wanted my first meeting with fae-kind to go down, not when I was supposed to represent the entire shifter community.

The woman didn't look at all distressed or apologetic about the make-out she'd interrupted. Her expression was blandly blank.

"I have a matter of some importance to relate to you," she said in a thin, shimmering voice.

Footsteps were thudding over the stone floor on either side of us. Nate appeared first, then Aaron and West, all of them slowing to a halt when they saw our visitor. Marco waved them all over, but I saw his jaw was still set a bit tight. He wasn't completely at ease, no matter how nonchalant he liked to appear.

How had the fae woman gotten past all of the alphas? Was there some other passage we'd missed—or had it been some kind of magic? It didn't seem wise to ask the guys right in front of her. I didn't need her knowing just how ignorant I was about all things supernatural.

West's lips had drawn back over his teeth in a wolfish snarl. His stance was completely tensed. "What are you doing here?" he gritted out.

Nate stepped closer, towering over the slip of a woman. I could tell from his pose that he was braced to shift into his grizzly form the instant he felt he needed to. Aaron set a hand on his arm, but the eagle shifter's eyes gleamed with a determined light. He might not want to rush into a confrontation, but he was ready for it.

"Apparently she has some important info to pass on," Marco said, and nodded to the fae woman. "So go on."

She cocked her head consideringly, taking in my

alphas. "I come with the intention to help. There is no need to be defensive."

"We'll judge that for ourselves," West said.

Aaron stepped forward, making a brisk motion toward the wolf shifter as if asking him to stand down. "We're listening," he said, his voice even but not friendly. "What is it you wanted to tell us?"

"We discovered one of your kind sneaking after you in the caves, carrying a weapon," the fae woman said. "One with no ties to any of your kin-groups. Clearly he had ill intentions."

A rogue. My back stiffened. "Where is he?"

"You don't need to worry about him any longer. We disposed of him in an appropriate manner."

She moved her hand in an arc through the air and conjured an image like a hazy video recording, floating in mid-air. A weasel scuttled along the wall of the cave. It had a small knife clamped in its jaws. A chill ran down my spine.

I recognized that animal. One of the rogues who'd ambushed us in the mountain pass had transformed into a weasel to flee. I was sure that animal was the same one. So he'd been tailing us through the cave, carrying yet another forbidden weapon. The moment we'd all had our guards down, even for a moment, I had no doubt he'd have tried to finish the job the group of rogues had attempted before.

Killing me.

In the conjured image, a fae man appeared in front of the weasel. His mouth moved, but the conjured display contained no sound. The weasel flinched and darted for a crevice. The man threw a bolt of searing light toward it. The bolt struck the weasel—and consumed it in a brief blaze. When the light faded, nothing of our enemy remained.

The fae woman gestured again, and the image vanished. She spread her arms as if to say, *There you have it.*

"We would rather have had him captured alive so we could have questioned him," Aaron said. He managed to keep his tone even, but his rasp had become more pronounced. And why shouldn't he be upset? The weasel shifter might have been our enemy, but the fae couldn't have been sure of his intentions. He'd been *our* business to deal with as we saw fit. And they'd just slaughtered him with a single swipe of magic.

What if they decided we deserved the same treatment?

"He was not inclined to cooperate, as you could see," the fae woman said. "My companion could feel the murderous intent in him. We believed we were doing you a kindness." She paused, and her filmy eyes glittered in a way that set my nerves on edge. "You are the alphas of the shifter-kin, are you not? And the long-missed dragon shifter."

I liked the way her gaze settled on me even less. Apparently the guys all had the same feeling, because they drew closer around me at the same moment.

"We are," Marco said. I guessed she must have been able to sense their status, maybe through the oath-scars on their hands. "And she is. And as far as we knew, no one has made a direct claim on this mountain. I hope we aren't intruding."

"Not at all," the fae woman said, but I thought her sheen jittered a little. "We venture into the mountains from time to time, but we don't consider them truly part of our home. There is room enough for both."

"So this is basically a vacation spot for you," Marco said. He raised his eyebrows at the cave around us. "You have interesting tastes."

"The landscape has qualities that appeal in their own way. I suppose you've noticed other signs of our presence on your travels."

"We didn't think you'd been here recently," Nate put in. "Otherwise we'd have reached out to you."

"Did you pass on word to your people elsewhere?" the fae woman asked. She gave us a demure smile. "I know we've had our disagreements in the past. If there will be more shifters arriving, it would be best for us to know they're here on your request. To avoid any awkward encounters."

Like a fae deciding to incinerate another shifter?

"We aren't expecting anyone to join us," Aaron said. "But please, if you come across another rogue lurking around, bring the matter up with us before taking any action."

The fae woman bowed her head in a way that didn't look all that apologetic to me. My skin prickled. Maybe the dragon shifters and the fae had worked together long ago, but right now I didn't trust them at all.

"Is there any particular reason you're here right

now?" West asked, his voice tight. He obviously shared my sentiments.

"We were simply passing by and noticed you doing the same." The fae woman tipped her head. "All four of the alphas and their long-lost mate up here together—*you* must be making this trip on a matter of some importance."

She said it as a statement, but the question was clearly implied. My hands clenched. She claimed she was helping us, but every sense I had screamed that she had other intentions. I had no interest in sharing my mother's story with her.

"Serenity is still adjusting to her new role," Aaron said. He was the only one who called me by my full name, the name my mother had urged me to keep secret the entire time we'd been in hiding, and sometimes it still felt as if he were talking about a stranger. Right now, faced with the fae, I appreciated the formality of it. "There aren't many places a dragon shifter can exercise her powers without needing to worry about discretion."

"I suppose your people must at least know you've traveled up here," the fae woman said. "They'll be awaiting your return."

"We'll be back soon enough," Marco said. I restrained a frown. What was she getting at?

Maybe it was time we started asking more of the questions. I didn't want to tell her much about Mom, but she might know things I didn't.

"My mother came up here at least once in the last several years," I said. "She liked to visit the mountains too. I don't suppose you 'passed by' her then?"

The fae woman pursed her lips. "I can't recall the last time I saw any dragon shifter in these heights. I can ask my companions if they have more knowledge."

That was an incredibly vague answer. And if she could tell the alphas were alphas just by sensing it, surely she'd picked up on the marks Mom had left behind on the walls. Maybe she just assumed we'd already seen those?

"It sounds as though you're more familiar with this mountain than we are in general," Aaron said. "Is there anything we should know for safe passage from here on?"

The fae woman's mouth curled into another smile, but this one looked even chillier than the last. "You're the five most powerful shifters alive. I'm sure there's nothing on this mountain that could threaten you. I suppose I shouldn't delay you in your journey any longer. We are moving on now, so I doubt our paths will cross again."

"Thank you for your rogue-cleanup services," Marco said.

"Our pleasure," the fae woman replied without any hint of irony. She stepped backward to where a thin stream of sunlight penetrated the cave ceiling. With a quick leap, her form wavered and vanished into the glow.

"Should we be... worried?" I asked, staring up toward the sliver of daylight. Was she still here, only invisible, or could we assume she'd completely left? I didn't want to talk too freely in case it was the former.

"We'll just have to wait and see," Aaron said, a little grimly. "Let's keep moving while we have the light."

CHAPTER 5

Ren

SOMEONE'S MOUTH was moving over my bare skin. Scorching it with hot breath and the graze of his teeth. My breath was already coming in sharp pants.

He kissed his way down my throat, between my breasts, and over my belly. His tongue scorched me everywhere it touched. His fingers trailed down my sides, even hotter than his mouth. They came to rest on my hips just as his face hovered over my sex.

A thrill of anticipation and need tingled through me. I arched up encouragingly, and he took me in his mouth.

His tongue slicked over my clit, sending sparks of bliss all through my body. I whimpered as he suckled harder. He was devouring my core as if he meant to swallow me whole, and I was all for it. I moaned, weaving my fingers into the soft, smooth strands of his hair. A deeper need swelled inside me. An ache to feel him inside me, all of him. To know he was mine and I was his, now and forever.

"Please," I murmured. "Please." I tugged at his hair, and he raised his head. West's dark green eyes gleamed. His lips curled with a satisfied smile, and—

I jerked awake, my heart thudding. The chilly mountain air cooled my flushed face. The weight of the thick sleeping bag enveloped me. I was completely covered up and completely alone. It'd only been a dream.

But fuck, what a dream. My panties were sopping beneath the leggings I'd worn to bed. The ache of need lingered deep in my belly. I had the urge to reach down and take care of things myself, but I wasn't *actually* alone in the tent. Marco lay on one side of me, with a murmur of breath that reminded me of the little meows sleeping cats made. And West, the real West—

I turned my head to look at him instinctively, as if to confirm he was definitely still the grouchy, standoffish guy I'd had to badger into even kissing me the other day. Although it'd been quite a kiss when he'd given in. My eyes found his form in the darkness, lying on his side a couple feet away from me.

But not asleep. Just enough of the light from the campfire outside seeped through the tent wall for me to make out his features. To see him staring right back at me.

My pulse skipped again as our gazes met. I expected him to pull his away, to roll over and shut me out. Instead his eyes stayed locked with mine. They didn't hold the same lustful warmth as in my dream, but a tingle crept over my skin all the same. His expression was tense, but I also saw the same hunger I had when he'd looked at me

41

naked after my shift. As if he were just a hair's breadth from reaching out and yanking me to him.

As if he'd woken up from the exact same dream I had. Suddenly I was sure that was what had happened. I could smell his arousal in the air, a waft of piney musk. But he was fighting it.

I wet my lips, and his gaze twitched down to my mouth. Before I could decide what to do about this weird but oh-so-tempting moment, Marco stirred at my other side. He scooted closer and nuzzled the back of my neck.

"Someone feeling the need for a little middle-of-the-night action?" he murmured in his languid voice. I guessed it wasn't just West's arousal scenting the air. My nerves hummed with anticipation. I needed *something*, that was for sure.

I arched into Marco encouragingly, and he kissed the crook of my jaw. The zipper of my sleeping bag hissed as he eased it down for better access.

I tipped back my head to offer more of my neck to him. Marco branded me with his hot mouth, drawing his body against mine. His hand traveled up under my shirt. He groaned when his fingers brushed over my unconfined breasts. He stroked them skillfully, tracing pleasure all through my chest, and I whimpered. My gaze slid back down to meet West's again.

He was still watching. His pupils had dilated, and I could hear the quickening of his breath in time with mine. My awareness of his desire turned me on even more. I gasped as Marco pinched one of my nipples.

"Tell me what you want, princess," he said huskily. "Anything at all. It's yours."

I didn't think I'd ever wanted anything more than for West to cross that gap between us and add his mouth and hands to the mix. Just the thought of it made me twice as wet between my legs. In that instant, my hormones overrode common sense. I reached out my arm toward West to beckon him over.

Before I'd even finished the gesture, West flinched. His gaze snapped away. "*Don't,*" he said, his voice thick with strain. He shoved off his sleeping bag and threw himself onto his feet. With a slap of the tent flaps, he'd stalked out.

Marco chuckled under his breath. "He'll come around, princess. Especially after he sees how good the rest of us have it. But don't worry, I can make you see stars all by myself."

He rolled me toward him and caught my mouth with his. The heat of his kiss washed over me. It was hard to think much about West when I had this much man right in front of me.

I kissed Marco back, letting all my need and desire spill into the places where our bodies touched. He let his hands slip lower, teasing over my stomach and tracing the waist of my leggings. When I kissed him harder, he dipped his hand right under the fabric. He cupped my sex, grinning against my mouth as I moaned.

His mouth claimed mine again. His tongue tangled with mine. His fingers stroked over the sensitive folds between my legs with increasing pressure. I clutched him, shivering with pleasure, riding his hand.

"That's right, princess," Marco murmured. "That's my girl." He kept up his gentle caresses as he kissed his way down to my chest and tugged my shirt up with his other hand. His breath spilled over my bare skin. He swirled his tongue around my breast before sucking the nipple into his mouth.

A little cry of pleasure burst from my lips. I felt ready to explode.

"You taste so good. I need to taste you everywhere." Marco gave my breast one more swipe and then ducked lower. I whimpered in dismay when his hand left my sex, but it was only to ease my leggings down. A second later, he'd lowered his face between my legs.

Like West in my dream. Fragments of that imagined intimacy darted through my head as Marco swirled his tongue over my clit. I gasped, arching up, and he licked lower, teasing my opening. Carried on the rising wave of bliss, I almost felt as if both he and West were there, my dream and reality merging into one. The ache in my belly came back, twice as strong. My hips bucked, wanting more. Wanting everything.

I gripped Marco's hair, but he didn't release his claim on my pussy. He laved my clit until I was trembling. One finger, then two tested my wetness and then slid up inside me. I moaned again as the pleasure rose higher.

Marco nipped me, just hard enough to send a brief spark of pain through the pleasure, and that tipped me over. I came, shuddering against his mouth. The orgasm washed over me, and the stars Marco had promised flashed behind my eyes.

Marco smiled and kissed my sex again as my tremors subsided. He eased up beside me, pulling my body flush against his, and brushed his lips against mine. My tart flavor lingered in his mouth. I pressed closer to him, sated and yet still hungry. The hard length of him bulged against the fly of his pants. His hips rocked against me as his hands caressed my ass, sending fresh sparks all through my nerves.

It would be so easy to peel off his pants and open myself to him. To solidify our mate-bond and tie us together for life.

"Ren," Marco mumbled against my mouth. I heard the wanting in his voice. An awful lot of me wanted it too. But as we rolled with him on top of me now, my gaze dropped to West's empty sleeping bag.

This whole encounter had started with the wolf shifter. With him and that scorching dream. And here I was getting down and dirty with Marco instead.

Could I really know *what* I wanted right now, in the heat of the moment? The mate-bond, it was for life. When I accepted it with each of the guys, I wanted to be absolutely sure, no room for doubts. No misguided lust clouding my thoughts.

Marco adjusted himself over me so our bodies aligned perfectly. His erection pressed between my legs. I was drowning in the heat of him.

I touched his cheek and eased him back after another kiss. He grinned down at me, his eyes so bright with longing that guilt twisted my stomach. The grin faltered when he took in my expression.

"Princess?"

I drew in a shaky breath. "I'm sorry. I don't think I'm ready. Not quite yet."

He couldn't hide the disappointment that darted

across his face before he schooled it into his usual cool nonchalance. He nuzzled my hand, his smile coming back. "Ren, I'm not going to push. But you understand why I want you so much, don't you? My lovely Princess of Flames. You have no idea how much you mean to me already."

The soft words brought a flutter into my chest. "You hardly know me," I couldn't help pointing out.

"I know you enough." He bent his head close to mine, not to kiss me but to whisper by my ear. The rich spicy-coffee scent of him filled my nose. My mouth practically watered.

"I know you're the most determined woman I've ever met," he said. "I know you'll do anything to defend the people you love. I know you've got a sharp enough tongue to rival mine sometimes. I've never cared about anyone as much as I care for you. You can take that as a promise."

The flow of his words against my ear left me tingling. He moved above me, and I almost whimpered at the feel of his cock, still hard against me. My fingers gripped his shoulders. He rocked against me gently, sending quivers through my core. It was getting hard to think again. So much of me was screaming for another release.

"And I hope you have at least a few positive feelings about me," Marco added lightly.

"I think that should be pretty obvious," I muttered, but that flippant answer didn't feel good enough. "It's not about you. This whole situation just—it still doesn't feel normal to me. I've never committed to anyone, let alone *four* guys in just a few days. You grew up knowing it'd be like this. I can't wrap my head around the idea that fast."

"I know, princess. I know." He stilled and kissed my cheek. "I'll wait. I just can't help wanting to start our lives together as quickly as possible now that I've found you."

My throat tightened a little at the emotion in those words. "I'll be ready soon," I said. "I'm getting there."

At least, I hoped I was. The feelings in my chest suddenly felt a lot more tangled. Lust was easy. Love... Was I really going to be able to handle giving my whole heart to all four of these guys, as drawn to all of them as I was?

CHAPTER 6

Marco

I'D BEEN through plenty of pain in my life. You named it, I'd probably been there at least once. But I'd never experienced any torture quite as exquisite as waking up next to my mate who still wasn't entirely my mate.

Ren was still sleeping. Her expression was soft and her hair a mess of dark brown waves spilling from the top of the sleeping bag. I wanted to kiss her gently like the angel she looked like—and I also wanted to pull her to me and ravish her until she agreed to finishing what we'd started and come so close to ending last night.

My cock hardened just remembering the feel of her. Her smell flooding my nose, her taste filling my mouth, the little cry she'd made as she came. I could take her even higher than that. All I needed was for her to give me the chance.

It was going to take time for her to come around.

That was understandable. What we'd all been waiting for across nearly two decades, she'd only had a few days to process. I was a feline, wasn't I? I knew how to give a person space.

As painful as that space might be.

I stretched on the hard ground, willing my erection to subside. That fae woman—thinking of her was a good mood killer. I'd bet if she touched my dick, it'd shrivel up like a fallen autumn leaf.

There, that did the trick. All cooled down below. I peeled off the sleeping bag and ducked out of the tent.

Nate had a pan sizzling over the fire. We'd brought a good stock of cured bacon, but even though it didn't need cooking, it tasted twice as good fried. The salty, meaty smell tickled into my nose. My stomach grumbled. I wasn't normally much of a hiker, and all this mountain climbing had left me ravenous.

If I couldn't devour Ren the way I wanted, at least I could have my way with breakfast.

"Where's our wolf and eagle?" I asked, sinking down by the fire and stretching out my legs. The smoke curled up toward a small gap in the cave ceiling above us. "And how long until you surrender some of that bacon?"

"You can have it now," Nate said with a hint of a smile. The bear looked more relaxed this morning, even though he'd been up the second half of the night on guard duty. He flipped a couple of strips off the pan with surprising grace and tossed them to me. I snatched them out of the air and dug in. The hot, crispy pork seared my tongue, but the sting was worth it.

"Biscuits," Nate added, tossing over the bag. The

49

doughy lumps didn't appeal half as much as the meat, but they made for good energy at the start of the day. Nate dug into one of his own as he tossed a few more strips of bacon onto the pan. "Aaron and West are taking a quick survey of the area farther down the cave in both directions. Aaron didn't want to be careless after yesterday."

Because of the fae woman or because of the weasel? Both were reason for concern. I tore a biscuit in half and shoved the rest of my bacon inside to form a rough sandwich. In a minute, I'd gulped that down and was reaching for another. Nate gave me a bemused look when I started eyeing the pan again.

"We *all* need to eat," he said. "Ren is still sleeping?"

I nodded. "I figured the princess deserved her beauty rest."

Nate bristled slightly, as if he thought I'd meant that remark as an insult. "She's been holding up well."

"Of course she is," I said, waving him down. Ren had been even less prepared for this kind of physical strain than the rest of us. And she'd shifted into dragon form twice that first day. I'd have let her sleep until noon without judging if I could have. But we did need to get to the end of this journey soon. The biscuits were already getting a tad bitter with staleness.

"West was sleeping by the fire when I got back from sentry duty," Nate said, with a prodding tone. "Instead of in the tent."

I shrugged. "You know how wolf boy is. He's still got issues with our Princess of Flames being anywhere near his personal space."

The canine alpha was an idiot. The mate we'd all been waiting our entire lives for had been right there in front of him, practically begging him to come to her, and he'd turned tail in the opposite direction. He had to want her just as much as I did. I couldn't understand that kind of self-denial at all.

Footsteps sounded on the rocky ground. Aaron came into view, his thoughtful expression perking up at the smell of the food. He ambled over to the fire and grabbed a piece of bacon right out of the pan. Show-off.

I eyed the eagle shifter as he hunkered down by the fire. What exactly had he done to make Ren choose him first? Choose him—and still hesitate about the rest of us. I was at least that bird-brain's equal.

"No reason for concern up ahead," he said. "At least not from what I saw."

"Not behind us either," West said, emerging from the shadows in the other direction. He flexed his neck with a crack of his joints. "Let's eat and get going. Where's Ren?"

"Coming, coming," a muttered voice carried from the tent. Our dragon shifter pushed past the flap, running her fingers through the rumpled waves of her hair. Even barely awake and dressed in wrinkled clothes, she was the most gorgeous specimen of womankind I'd ever seen. I took her in, enjoying the eyeful.

She lifted her head and sniffed. "Bacon again?"

"Take what you can get, Sparks," West said, his already gruff expression shuttering even more. Yeah, wolf boy had a few issues to work through. Too bad for him. That just left more room for me to make my moves.

51

Ren ambled over. "Oh, I'm not complaining. I'd eat nothing but bacon for the rest of my life if I wouldn't end up with scurvy." She sat down cross-legged between Aaron and me and hummed happily as Nate passed her a couple strips.

Even the way she crunched into the bacon was sexy enough to get me half hard again. Fuck, this mate-bond thing was brutal. In the most tantalizingly torturous way.

A much less pleasant sensation twisted in my gut. My body stilled. I frowned as my stomach gurgled and roiled. I didn't like the feel of that at all. What was going on with my innards all of a sudden?

"What's wrong, Marco?" Aaron asked, being Mr. Eagle-Eyes.

"Nothing," I said with a dismissive gesture. "Just a little—"

I'd been going to say it was just indigestion. But before I could get the words out, a feverish flush washed through my body. My stomach outright lurched, heaving up toward my throat. There was nothing I could do but spin around before I vomited the food I'd just eaten onto the ground.

Ren

Marco knifed over with a sickly gurgle. I jumped to my feet, my pulse hiccupping. My fingers dug into the biscuit I'd just taken. The salty flavor of the bacon went sour in my mouth.

The other guys sprang up to. Aaron ran to Marco's side. "I'm fine," the jaguar shifter protested, right before he gagged again, clutching his stomach. West eyed him, his stance rigid. Nate took a step toward him and stopped, his hand falling to his abdomen. A sudden sweat gleamed on his forehead.

"He's not fine," he said. "And I don't think I am either."

"The food," West snapped. He dropped down by the pack we'd filled with our meal supplies, leaning close to take in a deep breath. He smelled the package of bacon, tossed it aside, and reached for the biscuits. As he pressed his nose to the bag's opening, his eyes narrowed. He inhaled again, slow and careful.

"They're tainted," he said.

I hardly had a chance to wonder how or what exactly that meant. Nate barged around the fire and smacked the biscuit I'd been holding from my fingers. I blinked at him, shaking my stinging hand.

"Sorry," he said, his mouth twisting. "I just— I couldn't let you—"

He staggered over to the cave wall and sank down. Aaron's head had jerked toward West.

"What is it? How serious?"

"Some kind of toxin," West said. He pulled out one of the biscuits and broke it open to take another careful sniff. "A natural substance, not artificial. Hard to pick up if you're not looking for it. Which obviously was the point."

"They've been *poisoned*?" I burst out. "What are we going to do?"

"How many of these did you eat?" West asked Marco.

"A couple," Marco muttered. He wiped his mouth, his dark hair slanting over his hooded eyes. He kept his face averted as if ashamed—as if he thought I'd feel anything other than concern and sympathy seeing my mates in this state. My hands balled at my sides.

"I only had one," Nate said by the wall, his voice strained. A shudder ran through his sprawled legs.

"They're not laced very heavily," West said. "To make it harder for us to notice. You're feeling the effects, obviously, but I'd be surprised if it's enough to kill you."

Marco snorted. "Oh, *that's* comforting."

If he could still manage sarcasm, he couldn't be in absolute agony. But he was clearly feeling pretty wretched. His arm was wrapped tight around his belly. I looked from him to Nate, wanting to be with both of them, comforting them, at once. "Who could have done it? Who would have *wanted* to do it? Do you think—that weasel yesterday..."

West grimaced. "There's a faint scent that says mustelid to me. They all have that oily thing going on. I'd say he's our culprit, definitely."

That answered the *why*, at least. The rogues had wanted to attack us any way they could. And we didn't have to worry about more harm from that quarter, because the fae had taken care of that enemy yesterday. But... "*When* could he have done it? We all ate biscuits yesterday morning, and we were fine. They've been in the pack since then, haven't they?"

Aaron nodded. "And it hasn't been out of our sight."

"There were times when we weren't paying a lot of attention to the supplies," Nate pointed out. "While we were packing up the tent. During the lunch stop."

"You'd think we'd have scented the weasel himself if he came that close." West set down the bag of biscuits, his eyes narrowing. "It's almost as if he snuck around us by magic, isn't it?"

Aaron gave him a sharp look. "We're better off not making accusations where we have no proof."

"No," West agreed, straightening up. "But it's something to keep in mind."

Magic. Did he think the fae had helped the weasel shifter get to us? But even if they'd wanted to hurt us, why would they have killed their ally afterward and pretended to be ours?

I wasn't sure if it was safe to ask. The fae woman had said her people were on their way off the mountain, but if they'd resort to poisoning, we obviously couldn't trust anything they'd said. And the way she'd appeared out of nowhere—how could I be sure they weren't listening to our conversation right now?

An eerie prickling ran over my skin.

Marco pushed himself back toward the fire, away from the puddle of sick. Like Nate, he was sweating, his face grayed beneath the gleam of perspiration. His arm wobbled as it supported his weight. But his eyes were mostly clear.

I knelt next to him, gripping his shoulder in a way I hoped showed how much I cared about him. "You should rest until you feel better." I glanced over at Nate. "You too. I don't want you making yourselves any *more* sick than you already are."

My gaze moved to Aaron. He was the one who'd spent the most time studying. Maybe he'd gone through some medical books in his reading. "Is there anything we can do to help them recover quickly?"

Aaron's bright blue eyes were solemn. "Every poison has an antidote, but we're pretty short on supplies up here. And we can't be sure of exactly what poison it is. West, we brought the first aid kit from the car, didn't we? Do you have activated charcoal in there?"

West's gloom momentarily lifted. "Probably. We've had issues with drugs among the teen shifters, so we like to keep that on hand in case of an overdose. Let me find it."

As he shuffled through the packs, I went to Nate's side. The bear shifter leaned his head toward me when I touched the side of his rugged face.

"I'll be all right," he said, a little hoarsely. "The poison will just have to run its course."

But we were so much weaker while two of my alphas could barely sit up. I nuzzled his arm, my helplessness tearing me up inside. My mates needed me, and there was nothing I could do. Even my dragon form couldn't burn the poison out of them. And of course Nate had to act all stoic, as if my worrying was a bigger problem than him being fucking *poisoned*.

I gritted my teeth. If that weasel shifter hadn't already been sizzled up by fae magic, I'd have been tracking him down right now. And I wouldn't have stopped to ask questions either. A nice little dragon snack, that's what he'd have turned into.

West hurried over, carrying a jar of black powder. He scooped some onto a small spoon and offered it to Nate. "It tastes like crap, but it'll help pull the poison out of your stomach."

Nate gulped down the powder and made a face. He started to try to push himself onto his feet, and I caught his arm.

"No way. Take it easy for once. I need you getting better, not running yourself into the ground."

He eased back down, but hesitantly. "We shouldn't stay here very long. There were other rogues that got away. They might still be following us."

"Or others who want to do us harm," West murmured darkly.

"And we just lost a significant portion of our food supply," Marco put in. He'd stretched out on his back, his muscled chest rising and falling with halting breaths. "Well, I guess this trek just got a lot more exciting."

CHAPTER 7

Ren

THE OPEN AIR tingled over my wings. I swooped across the mountainside, reveling in the glide of my dragon's body. After so long cooped up in the caves, the sense of freedom made me giddy. Part of me longed to flap those wings as hard as I could and soar all the way around the towering peaks, but I reined my impulses in. I wasn't out here to have fun.

My sharp dragon eyes scanned the rocky terrain again. Aaron had been right to doubt the hunting possibilities up here. I hadn't spotted anything living at this level of the mountain.

He was following me now in eagle form, conducting his own search while keeping me in view. Just in case I lost control of my shift. I didn't exactly *like* having a babysitter, but it was kind of comforting all the same. I hadn't gotten a lot of warning the last two times I'd run out of energy and had to shift back.

I swerved around to glide lower down the slope, to where a few sparse trees and shrubs managed to cling on to the rock. The deepening evening dark hid my immense, scaled form from anyone who might have glanced up from the town below. All I could see of Sunridge was a faintly speckled glow amid the shadowed landscape between the mountains.

While Marco and Nate had been recovering, West, who seemed to have the sharpest nose out of all of us, had gone through the rest of our food stores. Along with the biscuits, we'd had to chuck a bunch of beef jerky and a bag of apples. My precious Doritos were safe, but they weren't going to get us very far.

So while hunting wasn't proving very fruitful, we didn't have much choice but to try. Once we'd started walking again, slower to accommodate the weakened guys, we'd been lucky to find a gap in the ceiling wide enough for my dragon shape to fit through. It'd been a tight squeeze.

My attention jerked back to the present. A shadow had moved amid the sparse brush. A large hare, hopping tentatively from one shrub to the next. Not much of a meal for five, but I'd take what I could get at this point.

I swooped down, extending my forelegs. The hare froze at the sound of my descent. At the last second, it decided running might be a better strategy. Too late. My taloned foot snatched it up, one claw severing its neck to stop it from squirming.

Killing it had been easier than I'd expected. Some

natural instinct had taken over. I remembered what West had said the other night after he'd killed a deer. *We're all predators here.* At the time I'd thought he was just talking about the alphas. But he could have meant me too.

I didn't ever want to be *used* to killing things.

My muscles were starting to twitch with the need to let go of this form. I'd held it for a while now, longer than the last two times, but I didn't want to push my luck. I shot up the mountainside toward the crevice I'd emerged through. Aaron circled around after me, a smaller rabbit in his own grasp.

The prickling dug deeper into my muscles. My dragon's jaw clenched. I had to hold on. If I transformed back into human form out here on the mountain slope, totally naked... If we were too far from the cave, even Aaron wouldn't be able to get me back in time before I froze to death. And then there would be no dragon shifters left at all.

I pushed my wings through the air. It no longer felt so exhilarating. I spotted my salvation up ahead. A thin stream of smoke trickled up into the cold evening air. I plunged toward it.

The rough rock edge scraped over my scales as I dove through. I transformed as I fell, hitting the ground on knees already partly human. The impact jarred my bones.

But I still had the hare, its thick fur soft between my clutching fingers.

Nate hustled over with my clothes. The bear shifter was still moving more sluggishly than usual, but he'd regained a healthier color as the day had gone on. The charcoal West had given him and Marco seemed to have helped a lot. I hated to think what might have happened if they'd eaten more of the biscuits. Or if we all had.

I let Nate drape my jacket over my shoulders to fend off the worse of the chill and then tugged the rest of my clothes on as quickly as I could. I was shivering before I was halfway done. I hurried over to the fire, where Nate had already brought the hare and Aaron's rabbit.

My eagle shifter was just pulling on his shirt. The glimpse of his well-muscled chest—seriously, was that an eight-pack?—disappearing under the fabric was enough to send a completely different sort of shiver through me. Okay, now I was warm.

Marco was lounging by the fire, looking a lot less pained now too. But I knew the poison had hit him harder than it had Nate, probably because he'd gotten a bigger dose of it. His mouth still twisted a little when he bent over to grab the granola bar West tossed to him. And his joking didn't have quite the same lightness as it usually did.

"Those rogues had better not mess with us again," he said flippantly. "I *really* have a bone to pick with them now. And a few I'd like to shove into various parts of their body. A nice sharp rib through the gut would be just the thing."

West rolled his eyes. He leaned over to poke at the fire. We were getting low on wood too, I knew. It'd been too heavy for us to carry very much, and we hadn't been able to scavenge any to replenish our supply since we'd entered the caves. Maybe I'd need to make a different sort of trip above ground tomorrow morning.

"They obviously didn't do that much damage to you," West said to Marco. "You're still shooting your mouth off just as much as always."

Marco gave him a baleful look. "It takes a lot more than a couple of tainted biscuits to take down the leader of all feline kin."

"We don't know what they'll try next." Nate dug a knife into the hare's pelt to skin it. "We'll have to stay extra alert on watch tonight."

"Do you really think we have to be worried about... people other than the rogues?" I ventured. I still wasn't sure how wise it was to mention the fae directly. West hadn't done more than insinuate that they might be involved this morning.

Aaron clearly realized what I meant. "There are treaties between all the major supernatural communities," he said. "Attacking the leaders from one community, unprovoked, would bring about major consequences. It would be a huge risk."

"If it could be proven who was involved," West muttered. "Just make it easier for someone else to do the job, and you can get off scot-free."

"Have relations between the different communities been so bad they'd *want* to get rid of us?" I asked.

Aaron shook his head. "I wouldn't have thought so. It's possible, but West is jumping to the most dire explanation, not the most likely."

"Easy to say when you can just fly on out of here if the going gets that tough, eagle boy," Marco said.

His tone was teasing, but I saw Aaron's jaw twitch. He'd told me a few nights ago how the other kin-groups tended to see the avians as something lesser—and therefore to see him as the least important of the alphas. He didn't buy into that belief, but off-the-cuff comments like that must still carry a bit of a sting. I knew he'd never leave us behind no matter how tough the going got.

"Except he wouldn't," I said. "We're all doing the best we can."

"The best we can would be to get out of this mountain already," West said. "I don't suppose you have any idea how much longer *that* is going to take, Sparks?"

I grimaced at the nickname, but my gut knotted at the same time. I'd still been feeling the internal tug toward whatever was waiting for us—but I had no idea how much farther we had to go. If I could have just raced ahead on my own...

But that would be stupid. And exactly what anyone trying to get rid of me would want. These attacks had always been about the dragon shifters first. The rogues wanted my line eliminated. My alphas had only gotten hurt because they stood in the way.

"It can't be that much farther," I made myself say. "There can't be that much more *mountain*."

"And tomorrow Marco and I should be able to keep up the usual pace," Nate said. He set the skinned carcasses over the fire. The flames licked up over the meat, sending a mouthwatering roasting scent into the air. "There's no point in stewing over things we can't know. We just prepare as well as we can, and we'll be ready for whatever happens."

I wished I could feel the same easy confidence. I

couldn't even be sure of holding a shift for more than ten minutes at a time.

But even if West's question had been a little harsh, he wasn't wrong. The four of them were here because of me, because of this quest Mom had sent me on. If Marco or Nate had gotten more than just sick that would've been on me too.

My fingers itched with nothing around to pilfer. Everything around me was an unappealing target.

Because it was all too close to being mine, I realized. Somewhere during the last few days, my mind had completely adjusted to the idea that the four guys around me and I shared an inexplicable connection, one that made them part of my inner circle—which until now had included only me, my mom, and Kylie. There was no relief in stealing from the people I trusted to be on my side.

The unease stayed coiled in my belly all through dinner. My hunger had faded, but I forced a decent portion of rabbit down, followed by a granola bar, just to keep my energy up.

Marco and West took the first guard shift. I went to help Aaron set up the tent while Nate finished securing the campsite.

As my fingers grazed Aaron's here and there, as he brushed past me to fix one of the poles, another kind of hunger started to well up inside me. The need to feel that connection between us, to remind myself that it was right for them all to be here with me.

When we ducked inside, I took his hand and pulled him down to sit on top of my sleeping bag with me. He gathered me in his arms and kissed me. In that moment, with his lips parting mine and the heat of his body against me, all my worries faded. I was here, where I was meant to be, with the men I was meant to be with.

I eased us down onto our sides on the padded surface, wanting to feel him against me from head to toe. He hooked his arm around me, his thumb teasing over the bare skin of my back just beneath my shirt. I quivered with pleasure and kissed him harder.

The tent flap rasped. I eased back from the kiss and glanced up. Nate had come in, his tall frame stooped to avoid toppling the tent. Heat flared in his dark brown eyes as he took us in, but he hesitated as if unsure whether to continue forward or head back out.

Suddenly just having Aaron with me didn't feel like enough. I needed more. I needed to be completely wrapped up in the bond of desire and affection that ran between all of us.

I'd almost given in to that urge with Marco and West yesterday. The guys thought it was normal. Why should I hold back?

I drew in a breath and held out my hand.

A smile split Nate's face. He hunkered down at my other side, pressing a kiss to the back of my neck. And just like that, I was surrounded by warmth.

The musky pepper of the bear shifter's scent mingled with the salty tang of my eagle. I inhaled it deeply and pulled Aaron into another kiss.

Two pairs of hands traveled over my body. Two sets of lips marked my skin. Aaron's tongue twined with mine as Nate nipped the crook of my shoulder. The bear shifter looped his arm over me to caress my breasts. Aaron's fingers traced over my waist and tugged my hips closer to his. The bulge of his erection pressed against me, tantalizingly hard. I arched into it with a whimper.

Nate eased up my shirt, and the eagle shifter pulled back to let the other alpha peel it right off of me. Then Aaron made quick work of my bra. I yanked at his own shirt, eager to see the hardened chest I'd only gotten a glimpse of an hour ago. He stripped it off, and Nate did the same with a chuckle behind me. When they both slid closer again, the heat between us, bare skin to bare skin, was outright burning.

Aaron claimed my mouth, cupping my bare breasts at the same time. The peaks pebbled with a single touch. Nate started kissing his way down my spine. Every press of his lips sent an urgent pang of bliss through me. I moaned and squirmed, the desperation for release—any kind, whatever I could get—building inside me.

Nate paused at the small of my back, flicking his tongue over the sensitive skin there. I whimpered encouragingly. Aaron teased my nipples into even stiffer peaks with a swivel of his thumbs. Every sweep of them across those tips stoked the flame of need inside me. Then Nate's hand slipped over my ass and between my legs.

I let out another moan, pressing into his touch. My panties felt soaked through. Could he feel how turned on I was even through my pants?

Aaron dipped his head to suck the tip of my breast into his mouth. Nate stroked my sex. A gasp slipped from my lips. The sensations of their combined attentions were overwhelming, but oh so good.

I rocked my hips, and my clit brushed Aaron's erection. All at once, I couldn't stand the longing anymore. I wrenched at his slacks, fumbling with the button. I yanked the pants partway down. Aaron groaned as I palmed his cock. The silky hard length of him pulsed against my hand.

"Serenity," he murmured. It sounded almost like a question. One I knew the perfect answer to.

"Inside me," I said around another whimper. "*Now*."

The two guys tugged down my pants together. Aaron rolled me over so I was facing Nate. As the bear shifter leaned in to kiss me on the mouth, my eagle stroked me between the legs from behind as Nate had before. He hummed happily as his fingers tested the moisture there. He dipped them into the hot, slick center of me, and I gasped against Nate's mouth. Then the head of Aaron's cock rubbed over my opening. I shuddered with pleasure, on the verge of losing it already.

He eased inside me with a slow, steady thrust that sent a flare of pleasure through me. I'd never felt so complete as when he filled me. But Nate was still there with me too, kissing me through my moans, caressing my breasts and then reaching down to massage my clit.

Aaron plunged deeper into me from behind, holding my hips to steady them. The pleasure inside me swelled with each pump of his cock and each motion of Nate's hands, until it was almost unbearable. I had to give more of it back.

I groped for Nate's jeans. He undid the fly with one

quick movement. His hips jerked toward me as I slipped my hand inside. My fingers closed around his cock, just as hard and even bigger than Aaron's to match the bear shifter's massive frame. I moaned just at the feel of it.

Gripping the silky skin tightly, I slid my hand up and down in time with Aaron's rhythm inside me. Precum beaded on the tip. I slicked it down over his length. Nate groaned and crushed his mouth against mine.

Aaron adjusted our angle so he filled me even more deeply. His shaft brushed that special spot inside me, and I felt myself careening toward the edge of total bliss. I squeezed Nate even harder, pumping faster, and he bucked his hips toward me. His kisses turned ragged. So did my breath. He rubbed my clit one last time, and my orgasm burst inside me like a firework.

I came apart, clutching Nate's cock, and he followed me. A hot liquid spurt hit my stomach. Then Aaron was coming too, with a few last jerks of his hips. He bit my shoulder as he spilled himself inside me. That mingling of pain and pleasure was enough to send me right back over the edge.

We collapsed against each other, gasping and boneless. Nate brushed the sweat-damp hair from my forehead and pressed a kiss there. "Our dragon shifter," he said, so tenderly my heart started to ache.

Aaron grabbed his sleeping bag and pulled it over us like a blanket. I fell asleep like that, cuddled up between two of my mates, able to forget just for a little while that the hardest part of our journey might lie ahead of us.

CHAPTER 8

Ren

"I THINK WE'RE GETTING CLOSER," I said, and then winced at how stupid that comment sounded. Of course we were getting *closer*, or all this walking was for nothing. What I really wanted to say was that we were *close* now. Over the course of the morning's hike through the cave, the tug inside me had strengthened into a yank. But I wasn't sure enough of what *close* meant to want to risk saying it, in case I was wrong. I could already imagine the look West would give me.

"For a place the fae apparently use as a summer home, it could really use better lighting," Marco said dryly. We'd left the last of the crevices in the ceiling behind a couple hours ago. Now the only light glowing off the rough walls was the beam of the flashlight Aaron was carrying.

"Is that something the fae do a lot?" I asked. It

seemed safe enough to ask general questions about them. "Move around between different homes?"

"Not unless they have specific business there," Aaron said. "Each of them usually has an affinity for one particular tree or pond, and their magic is weakened if they're away from it very long."

"If this mountain is special to the dragon shifters, it could have some meaning for the fae too," Nate pointed out.

I thought about that memory I'd had, talking about the fae with Mom. "Have you heard anything about the dragon shifters and the fae... working together, or associating with each other somehow?"

Aaron frowned. "I haven't come across anything referring to a collaboration in the research I've done into our history. But that doesn't mean it never happened. There's plenty the dragons have kept to themselves. Why?"

"Oh, I just remembered my mom saying something about that. But she didn't know any details either, from what she told me." When I wasn't even five yet. How much more might she have shared with me if I'd known the truth when I was older?

The pain of that loss returned with a dull ache. It'd been seven years since I last saw her, but following her trail had made me feel as if she'd only just slipped from my grasp.

"It doesn't matter what dragon shifters might have done once upon a time," West said darkly. "*You* should steer clear of them."

"If they come to the mountain regularly, one of them

might have seen my mom while she was here," I pointed out. "Even talked to her."

He shook his head without meeting my gaze. In the dim light, his deep green eyes looked even more shadowed. "It doesn't matter. They won't tell us anything unless they can use it to their advantage over us. Trust me. The only fae I like is one that's at least a hundred miles away. Or dead."

There was a rough note in his voice, beneath the more typical bitterness. I peered at him from the corner of my eye as we tramped on. He'd obviously had personal dealings with the fae in the past. Dealings that had caused *him* a lot of pain. I wanted to ask more, but I had the feeling he'd bite my head off for prying.

None of the other alphas had argued with him. Even if they didn't have the same hate for the fae, they mustn't have found his comments all that inaccurate either.

I shivered and rubbed my arms through the padded sleeves of my jacket. In that case, I hoped those shiny beings were now far, far away from here too.

"I guess I've got a lot of work ahead of me when we're done all this running around," I said.

Nate stepped closer and took my hand in his large one. The smile he gave me brought back the memories of what we'd gotten up to in the tent last night with a flush of warmth. "We'll be right there beside you, figuring things out together."

West made a wordless noise of dismissal. My temper flared. Why did he have to make it seem as if he was offended by even the slightest suggestion that I was worthy of the role I'd inherited? I'd been hiking up this mountain right along side him. Couldn't he cut me a little slack?

"So what exactly are you planning on doing if you throw away tradition and any hope of making this mate thing work, Mr. Wolf Man?" I demanded. "Annex the canine shifters from the rest of the shifter community? That doesn't sound like it's going to help anyone."

West finally turned his penetrating gaze on me. "I don't think you know enough about our community to have any idea what will help or not. When we're finished this ridiculous questing, maybe I'll get to see what you're really made of as a dragon shifter."

Maybe you should open your eyes, because I've shown you plenty already.

I bit back the snappy retort, swallowing hard. West wanted me to argue with him. Wanted me to give him excuses to keep antagonizing me. As if it were *my* fault that my mother hadn't taught me anything about the shifters. Or that the rogues had slaughtered my fathers and sisters to force us into going on the run in the first place.

Another memory, a fragment from long, long ago, rose up, so vivid the rest of the cave fell away. I was sitting on my mother's lap while she brushed my hair, which was knotted from a scramble through the woods with my sisters. She tsked her tongue as she worked through a tangle.

"You're lucky I believe in letting children run a bit wild. Otherwise we'd have rules about rolling down hillsides and dangling from trees."

My four-year-old self looked up at her with wide

eyes. "You could do that, couldn't you? You get to make the rules for all the shifters."

Mom laughed gently. "Not exactly. Not all by myself. Your fathers and I decide what's best for the community together."

"Indeed we do," my tiger shifter father had said, sauntering into the room. My other dads followed him. They stood around my mother and me, enveloping both of us both in an aura of familial love.

In the present, I blinked hard at the tears that had started to well in my eyes. My throat had tightened. So much the rogues had stolen from me. I'd barely gotten to know my fathers at all. How much would *they* have taught me?

But I knew how much they'd loved my mother. That was what the mate-bond between the alphas and their dragon shifter was meant to look like.

I raised my chin, pushing down the pang of loss. If West really believed I'd be a total disaster, he wouldn't still be here. He'd have forsaken me as his mate and taken off to find one he liked better. I just had to keep reminding myself of that.

Aaron's flashlight beam caught on a claw-shaped scar on the wall up ahead. A deeper scrape than Mom had left before. For a second I wasn't sure if this one had been made by her or something else, but as soon as I came up beside it, her energy tickled over my skin. The sense of her presence—and a thicker emotion. I let go of Nate's hand to touch the marks, and a jab of distress jolted through my body.

I paused, my fingers twitching toward my palm as if

echoing the sweep of her talons. She'd been upset when she'd scratched this mark. In pain or afraid. What had happened to her here? How had anyone even known she'd come up this way? She'd been so good at covering her tracks...

Nate hovered behind me. "What's the matter, Ren?"

"My mother," I said. "When she came through this part of the cave, something was wrong. She was upset. But I can't feel why."

"I don't see how we can get much more careful than we already are," Marco said. "Whatever comes, we'll handle it, princess. She shouldn't have had to come up here alone."

No, she shouldn't have. I bit my lip, but I forced myself to keep walking. The sooner we got to the end of this journey, the sooner I'd know what had happened to her. At least, I sure hoped so. If all it led to was another clue to follow, my dragon fire might come out in frustration.

That end might be coming up even sooner than I'd guessed. The light caught on a bend in the passage. As we came around it, the tug inside me yanked even harder than before. I stumbled, losing my breath. The second I caught my balance, my feet darted forward across the uneven ground, as if pulled from my control. I knew I could rein them in if I'd wanted to—but I didn't really.

"We're almost there. It has to be close now," I said.

The guys picked up their pace too. Light twinkled above us. I glanced up, thinking we must have come under another crevice to the outside world. Instead I saw crystalline stalactites glinting overhead, reflecting the artificial glow. A faint vibration emanated off them, quivering into my skin. Making me even more energized.

Almost there. Almost there.

I adjusted my pack's straps on my shoulders and pushed myself into a lope. That pull was reeling me in as if I were a fish on a line, but I was totally okay with that. I was ready for this trek to be done.

So it was my fault, really, that I was at the head of our procession at that moment. My fault that it was my feet the ground trembled under. I slowed as an eerie creaking sound resounded through the cave. The rock beneath my feet felt suddenly insubstantial, as if I'd stepped out onto a thinly frozen lake.

And then it cracked, exactly like the ice I'd just been picturing.

The ground fractured and started to fall away. My shifter reflexes kicked in not a second too soon. I threw myself forward.

The creaking rose into a full-bodied groan that reverberated through the cave. The pack dragged at my shoulders. Each time my feet hit the ground, the rock kept crumbling. I scrambled on. There was nothing I could do but run and hope I found a solid spot before I fell too.

My foot slipped, and I nearly crashed onto my knees. With a yelp, I heaved my body through the air as far as I could manage. I stumbled, caught my balance—and realized the ground had steadied.

"Ren!" someone shouted behind me, and someone else said, "She's okay, let her get her bearings." I turned cautiously, not quite trusting the stone beneath me yet. My jaw went slack.

Between me and my alphas, some ten feet of the cave floor had dropped away into a jagged chasm. I was standing just a couple feet from its edge.

I crept closer to peer into its depths. Nothing but darkness showed below. It was so deep I hadn't even heard the clatter of the crumbling rock hitting the bottom.

I'd almost hit that bottom. My stomach knotted. If I'd reacted any slower...

"Are you all right, Ren?" Nate called to me.

I nodded, still lost for words.

Marco gave an exasperated chuckle. "Because we really needed more excitement on this trip. All right, I'm not jumping that *with* luggage. Good thing we didn't pack anything breakable."

He shrugged off his pack and tossed it over the chasm. It landed with a thump. The other guys followed suit. I thought they might strip down to take the leap in their animals forms—possibly I was looking forward to that view—but I guessed shifter strength made the jump not too much of a challenge even in human bodies. Two at a time, they took a running start and sprang across the chasm.

Nate's brawny body hit the ground near me with a thud, and one last creak carried through the cave. The hairs on the back of my neck rose. I studied the edges of the chasm in the dim light as the guys dusted themselves off.

"How did that even happen?" I said. "It doesn't make

sense. A big gap like this wouldn't just *appear* with a tiny bit of rock over top. It's almost like it was..."

"A trap?" West filled in. "How long did it take you to figure that out, Sparks?"

I glared at him, but Aaron spoke up before my tongue got away from me. "It was definitely purposefully constructed. You said you could feel we're almost at the place your mother wanted you to reach, Serenity. A place that holds some kind of important power. It's possible there's magic protecting that place and the 'trap' was meant as a test of worthiness or determination."

"Or it's possible we've got some magical 'friends' unhappy we didn't die of poison," Marco said. "I'm starting to come around to wolf boy's point of view, as much as it pains me to admit that."

"Is there any way to tell what kind of magic was used?" I asked. Fae or otherwise.

Aaron shook his head. "It would have been beneath the layer of rock, holding it in place. So it fell away at the same time." He glanced at me. "But we made it past. You kept your head and got yourself out of there. Whatever power your mother wanted you to have, no one's going to stop you from getting to it, are they?"

"No," I said with a fresh burst of resolve. "So let's get a move on before we have to deal with anything worse."

CHAPTER 9

Nate

As I HEFTED my heavy pack from where I'd tossed it across the chasm, a splinter of pain shot through my chest down to my gut. I set my jaw, trying not to let the discomfort show on my face.

Even with all the rest I'd gotten yesterday and the slow pace we'd set after, the poison was still in my system. Still making me weaker than I should have been. I hated it. We might have gotten all the way to the end of this cave yesterday if we could have kept up our usual pace. Hell, if I'd noticed the off smell in the biscuits when I'd first grabbed one, I could have stopped Marco from eating them too.

I'd been complacent, and my mate was suffering because of it.

Ren was taking it all in stride. She adjusted her own pack against her back and smiled at me when she caught me looking at her. That quick gesture warmed me even with the twist of pain and guilt in my gut. Remembering her hands on me last night, her soft sighs of pleasure, the sweet taste of her skin...

Okay, that line of thinking wasn't going to help her either. Someone was out to sabotage our journey here—to kill us if they could. They'd literally torn the ground out from under us. I had to stay focused on the present, on defending Ren from our enemies. How could I be worthy of our mate-bond if I didn't?

If I'd waited all this time only to lose her now... I couldn't stand that thought. It made me feel sicker than the poison had.

Marco shot one last glance down the chasm and sauntered over. "I say we send bear boy ahead from here on," he said in his annoyingly jaunty tone. "If the floor holds under all that bulk, the rest of us won't need to worry."

West snorted. I glowered at Marco. "I'm happy to take the lead if you're a scaredy cat."

"Ooh," he said, grinning. "The bear got in a burn. Not bad, Nate."

Ren rolled her eyes. "Come on, guys. *I'll* take the lead if the rest of you are going to stand around debating it."

She moved to set off, and I strode ahead of her. For the first few steps, I wasn't aware of much except the need to assert my intentions and Marco's mocking chuckle. Then a faint scent reached my nose that didn't fit the cold rock around us.

I stopped, holding out my arm. "Stay back.

Something's not right."

West came up beside me as I inhaled again. His wolf's nose was the strongest out of all of us, but I could hold my own in that area when I concentrated. A faintly musky smell lingered in the air—something living. Something animal.

And we hadn't seen a single animal since we'd descended into this cave, other than our glimpse of that weasel the fae had taken care of.

"You're right," West said with a frown. He stalked a little farther ahead, scanning the cave around us. I wasn't going to be left behind. I followed him, testing the air myself. If anything, the scent got fainter. I turned and paced back the way we'd come. Ren watched me, her brow knit with concern. My stomach twisted tighter, seeing her worry.

"It's strange," I said. "It's strongest right around here. Whatever animal left that smell, it must have stopped here for a while. But then where did it go? We didn't pass anything on our way here."

"There's nothing I can pick up farther this way," West said from the spot where I'd left him. "It's so faint I can't get a clear read on it. Maybe it's old."

He sounded doubtful, probably because it didn't smell stale to him any more than it did to me. The faintness was more as if it'd been washed over somehow to try to remove the scent, with just a few lingering traces remaining. And that would mean someone had tried to cover their scent trail on purpose, so we wouldn't catch on. My shoulders tensed. You couldn't get much more suspicious than that.

"Can you tell what kind of animal it was?" Aaron asked.

I shook my head. It didn't really matter. If even a little weasel could pose a threat, we couldn't trust anything.

"We should walk close together," I said, motioning the other alphas over. "All of us around Ren, so there's no way anyone can get at her without going through us. If the rogues are planning another ambush, we have to be ready."

"I don't need a human shield," Ren protested. "Why don't we just—"

With a snarl, a blur of fur shot through the air toward her from the wall above. A bellow of warning broke from my throat. I leapt in front of my mate, pushing her backward and bracing myself to shift to meet the threat.

Ren

The force of Nate's shove sent me stumbling back toward the wall. I gritted my teeth, feeling my dragon wake up with a scrabble of claws in my chest. *No* one got to push me around, not even my mates.

What the hell was even happening? The flashlight had fallen after the snarl I'd heard. Its light rotated around the cave as it spun. It caught on Nate, already shifted into his grizzly bear form. He was trying to pin down a spotted wildcat that had come out of nowhere. It kept squirming out from under his paws. Aaron's eagle dove down to add his talons to the mix.

Across from them, West's wolf and Marco's jaguar were facing off with a big, black weasel-like creature my mind vaguely registered as a wolverine. It hissed and snapped at them with razor-sharp fangs.

Nate gave the wildcat a smack as it clawed at him. The impact sent it careening over the edge of the chasm. The last I heard was a feline shriek as it plummeted into the depths.

A harsh pant of breath behind me made me spin around. Not a second too soon. A coyote lunged at me, teeth snapping at my throat. I barely managed to dodge out of the way before it took a chunk out of me.

The coyote's lashing paws scraped across my arm, drawing blood through the sleeve of my jacket. It landed and whipped around with a gnash of its teeth. The flare of anger inside me grew hotter, and not just for myself. Back in the shifter village, two coyotes had savaged Kylie while their wolfish leader had attacked me. I had no doubt at all that this asshole was one of them.

I clasped hold of that fiery fury and wrenched it free. My body burst from its clothes, expanding into dragon form.

The coyote flinched back with a startled whine as I loomed over it. Fire bubbled up my throat. I opened my mouth to fry the attempted murderer back to kingdom come—

—and Nate charged between me and the coyote. The grizzly was only half as tall as my dragon's body, but he managed to block my aim completely.

I swung my sinewy neck, determined to take a snap at my attacker. Nate growled from deep in his chest and tackled the coyote first. They rolled, biting and swiping. I clenched my jaw, knowing I couldn't bring out the flames without roasting my bear alpha too.

Damn it. Why couldn't he let me handle one thing by myself?

I swung around to check on the other guys, my scaled shoulders brushing the cave wall. There wasn't much room for me to maneuver in here.

The wolverine was just making a dash between West and Marco. Marco cut it off at the last second, battering its eyes with both paws and heaving it onto its side. West leapt over with a snap of his teeth.

Aaron dove down, placing a threatening set of talons over the wolverine's neck. He meant to trap it in the hopes it would shift back into human state so they could question it, I had to guess. But the wolverine wasn't willing to face that consequence.

With a grunt, it wrenched its head up, stabbing the eagle's claws through its neck. Blood gushed out. Its furred body slumped. Aaron gave a cry and flapped away.

Nate pounded the coyote's head against the ground with one thick paw. The nimbler animal shuddered and scrambled away. I lunged toward it, smoke curling through my mouth.

My dragon's gaze locked with the coyote's. A totally human panic flashed through its eyes. I hesitated, wondering if there was some way I could restrain it without killing it. Before I could think of one, the coyote hurled itself over the edge of the chasm. It plummeted out of sight after its ally.

I stared at the gap, hot breath rasping in my throat. My hold over my dragon form trembled. I let myself collapse back into my human body.

The frigid air closed in around me again with a prickling ache. I scrambled for my jacket, the only thing I'd managed to cast off before I'd gotten far into the shift. The rest of the clothes I'd been wearing were shredded. I tugged the jacket around me, wincing as it brushed over the scratches on my arm. My shifter body would heal them quickly, but not *that* fast.

The guys were all shifting back too. My eyes caught on a blotch like a scar on West's leanly muscled chest that glowed with a faint reddish light. Then my gaze dropped to the limp body of a middle-aged man with a wiry beard that lay where the wolverine had died. Blood pooled around his head and shoulders.

Marco nudged the corpse's leg with his foot and grimaced. "So much for getting some answers out of these assholes."

My mind leapt back to the coyote flinging itself to its death. My stomach clenched. "They decided it was better to die than be caught. The rogues are pretty dedicated to their cause, aren't they?" Their cause, which was seeing me and any other dragon shifters that might be left dead.

Another thought struck me with a deeper horror. "They must have something to protect, then, right? There must be other rogues out there with other plans. Why else would it matter if we questioned them?"

"They could have been too ashamed of what they've gotten themselves involved with to want to face the consequences," Aaron said. "But you're probably right. We can't assume the rogue threat is finished." He glanced around. "I hope that's the last we see of them on this mountain, though."

"There weren't very many that survived the ambush," West said, already pulling his shirt over the strange scar I'd noticed. "What I want to know is where they came *from*. It looked like they practically fell from the ceiling."

I stepped closer to the wall, peering up at it. Aaron picked up the fallen flashlight and pointed it where I was staring. A slice of deeper shadow cut into the rock just below the ceiling.

"There's a ledge up there," I said. "They got up there somehow. Trying to stage another last ditch ambush." I guessed we were just lucky I'd melted all the guns this group had during their first attack.

"*Somehow,*" West repeated. "Yeah, I wonder about that. Maybe the same 'somehow' that created the trap in the floor?"

"It doesn't matter now," Nate said firmly. "What matters is getting to the power Ren's mother pointed us to, and then getting Ren out of here before anyone else comes after us."

He strode over to me, his head high as if he saw himself as some kind of knight in shining armor. The anger I'd felt earlier flickered back up.

"Getting us *all* out," I said. "I don't need special treatment. And I *really* don't need to be treated like a weakling."

Nate blinked "What are you talking about?"

I waved my hand toward the chasm. "You were so busy trying to 'protect' me a few minutes ago that you got in my way when I was about to blast that coyote to bits."

His expression tensed. "It's our job as your mates to—"

"No," I said, cutting him off. There was no room for argument here. Either he accepted my point or he didn't. "From what I've heard, it's your job to stand beside me. Not in front of me, like I'm some wimp who needs to be sheltered. I can shift now. I can shift into a freaking dragon." I pointed to the bite mark on his arm. "If you hadn't run in there, you wouldn't have had to get hurt. I could have handled it *better* than you did."

The stiffness left Nate's face, leaving only a stunned blankness. "Ren," he said, his voice quieting. "I didn't mean— Of course I know how strong you are."

My anger eased off. I knew he hadn't meant to offend me. "Okay," I said. "Then treat me like you know it. I'm not a china doll. Go ahead and look out for me—but let me look out for you too. That's how it's supposed to be, isn't it?"

He inclined his head, a faint flush of shame coloring his cheeks. Marco cleared his throat. "If we're done with the dressing down, deserved as it might be, can we get moving? I'm liking this vacation less and less with every new development."

"No kidding." I turned toward the passage ahead. A glimmer caught my eye, there and then gone. My heart leapt. "I think it's almost over."

CHAPTER 10

Ren

As MUCH AS I wanted to run through the cave toward
the beckoning glimmer, I held my legs in check this time.
I didn't want to be caught unprepared by another booby
trap. But the tug dragged at my chest and that hint of
light called to me, propelling me onward as fast as I'd let
myself walk.

The light brightened as we got closer, but it didn't
expand. I realized why soon enough. The passage ahead
of us narrowed into a slit so thin Nate was going to have
to walk sideways to squeeze through it. The light was
emanating from beyond it.

As I stepped through the opening, the light flared so
bright that my vision filled with white. It didn't sting my
eyes, though, only filled them with a faintly tingle.

I blinked the brilliance away. I'd come into a large,
round room where the stone walls and floor were

completely smooth. A pedestal stood in the center of the room. A clear crystal nearly the size of my head rested in its rocky hold. The light and a faint warmth glowed from within the crystal. The glimmer danced like a flame as I stared at it.

The tug inside me had fallen away. This was where it'd been leading me to. This was where I was meant to be.

I eased forward with a few careful steps. Shapes were carved into the pedestal's base. I bent down to examine them, holding my breath in awe.

The etchings showed the forms of dragons and other figures that looked almost human. But not quite. They were a little too tall and a little too slim to look exactly right. Like the fae woman we'd met below in the caves—like the fae man I'd seen my mother talking to.

The dragons and the fae stood side by side, sometimes touching, sometimes facing one another. In one depiction, a fae figure sat astride on a dragon's back. There was little detail to the faces, but all of the pictures gave me a friendly vibe.

I brushed my fingers over the fine grooves in the stone. "I think this must be something the dragon shifters and the fae created together," I said. "And that must have been a very long time ago, if there's no record of them spending time together."

Aaron nodded, coming up behind me. I circled the pedestal to give him room, and my gaze fell on not just pictures but words carved into the other side.

Between fae and draco, a power we birth, to give the

clearest sight. To be taken in a time when no other power can set the world right.

A shiver ran through me, reading the words. Above them, the images showed a figure lifting the crystal, then dropping it. In the last etching, a jagged flare exploded up from it over the figure.

That was what I had to do? *Smash* that crystal? I wasn't even sure what this power *was*. And the thought of even touching the glowing crystal made me nervous.

It had been waiting here for centuries. Was it really meant for *me*?

Mom had thought so. She'd made it almost this far. From what she'd said in her vision, she must have intended to bring the crystal back for me to take its power. All those trips away from home, I had to assume she'd been checking up on the shifter community. Seeing how they were getting by without us. What she'd seen, the disarray the alphas had told me about, had driven her here. To this desperate measure.

Maybe in a time when all the supernatural communities were in conflict, when rogue shifters had succeeded in nearly eliminating dragon-kind, we did need to turn to something greater.

It didn't matter what I was getting into. We'd come this far. I had to take this final step, or the whole journey had been for nothing.

West stalked around the room warily, but he didn't make any comment. Marco ambled over beside me to read the words for himself. Nate stayed by the door as if standing guard—and maybe also keeping a little distance from me after my outburst. I didn't regret anything I'd said, but I could feel his unhappiness from across the room. It pained me.

As soon as I got this over with, we could move on. And no one would be able to claim I wasn't powerful enough to hold my own.

I felt all of my alpha's eyes on me as I lifted the crystal from the pedestal. The faceted surface was glossy and hard as glass, but even warmer than the air around it. I gave in to the urge to hug it to my chest. The flickering heat licked over me, beckoning. Wanting to reach all the way into me.

My heart thumped. I raised the crystal to the level of my forehead. The light inside sparkled with a rainbow of colors. My chest tightened. I braced myself and dashed the crystal on the stone floor by my feet.

Light exploded up over me with an even sharper rush of heat. A searing energy rippled through my skin and into my bones. My pulse stuttered, and my mouth went dry. Hell, that was intense.

The energy flared right over my eyes from the inside out. The room around me faded into a gleaming haze. Through that haze, a silhouetted figure emerged.

"Greetings, worthy one," she said as the thrumming energy wrapped tighter and tighter around me. "The flame of truth is yours. Burn to destroy or burn away lies to get at what is real: The choice will be yours. Now go forward!"

She vanished into the light. The energy contracted into me with a jolt. Its burning ran all the way through my chest, prickling but not outright painful.

The haze in my eyes started to clear—but I couldn't

see the guys standing around me. Within the fading light, another vision appeared.

My mother strode into the room. My heart leapt, but then I noticed that she looked just as she had in my other vision of her from seven years ago. The same clothes, the same age. This was the past, not the present.

Her hair was rumpled and her cheeks smudged, but her eyes gleamed with determination. Her gaze settled on the crystal—the image of it that had reappeared as part of this vision.

"There," she whispered, as if hesitant to disturb the peace of this space. She stepped toward the pedestal—toward the spot where I stood beyond it. I swallowed hard, clenching my hand against the impulse to reach out to her.

She couldn't see me. This had all already happened. But she seemed so close.

Mom extended her hands toward the crystal. Her fingers were just about to close around it when something made her head jerk around. I hadn't heard anything, but the vision didn't seem to contain any sound at all. Just the rush of energy pulsing past my ears.

All at once, a crowd of other figures poured into the room as if straight out of the walls. At least a dozen slim, shimmering fae. One of them rushed between Mom and the pedestal. He shoved her backward with a spark of magic. His lips moved, but I couldn't make out the words.

Mom said something back—something angry, from the flash in her eyes. One of the other fae shook his head. A fae woman stepped forward with a sweep of her arm toward the doorway.

My mother's jaw tightened. I felt her starting to shift before her body had even twitched with the beginnings of the transformation. But the fae felt it too. At the same time, several of them, all around her, hurled glinting blasts of magic at her.

The blasts hit Mom with a burst of sparks. She staggered, faltering in her attempt to shift. With her arms raised defensively, she whirled around, but the fae were already whipping more of their glittering magic toward her. It smacked into her body, driving her to her knees.

A cry caught in my throat. My legs burned to run to her, as if I could help. I tried to shift them, and my feet stuck to the floor. There was nothing I could do but stand here and watch this piece of history play out.

Mom wasn't beaten yet. She pushed herself to her feet and lunged at one of the fae. Her face started to transform, scales dappling her skin, a flicker of dragon fire darting from her mouth.

The fae woman winced, but there were too many others. Before Mom could shift any farther, they caught her in another crashing wave of magic.

She fell again, this time onto her side. Her chest shuddered as she tried to breathe. Her lips moved with more words I couldn't hear. Then the fae man who'd blocked her way to the pedestal stepped closer. He clapped his hands and threw a spike of shimmering energy straight at Mom's head.

She crumpled, her body slumping against the floor. I choked on a sob. The fae looked at each other, a resolved expression crossing all their faces. One by one, they raised their hands over Mom's form. One stream of light, and then another, and then another, poured down at her.

The edges of her body shimmered, and then slowly started to disintegrate. My stomach turned. I couldn't stand still any longer. It didn't matter that this horrible moment was already done and over, seven years past. I *had* to stop this.

The muscles in my legs bunched to wrench my feet from the floor with every shred of strength in me, to run to her—but my joints locked. A vise seemed to clamp around my lungs.

You must watch, a faint voice echoed in the back of my head. *Watch and witness.*

So I did. I watched, my eyes getting hotter and hotter, as the fae's magic ate away at my mother's body. I longed to look away, to not have to see this slow destruction, but at the same time it did feel as if it was my duty to witness it. To acknowledge what had become of my mother—and who had done it to her.

When her body had completely faded away, the fae stepped back. The man who seemed to lead them had his mouth set in a grim line, but he brushed his hands together as if this had been nothing more than a brief bit of work. They wisped away into the walls again.

The vision fell away from me. The room came back into focus. My legs wobbled, and I clutched at the pedestal to keep my balance.

Marco and Aaron, still close by, each clasped one of my shoulders. Their presence steadied me, but my eyes were already full of tears. I inhaled with a hitch.

"What happened?" Nate said, moving from the

doorway. "For a few minutes there, you looked like you were in another world."

"I saw what happened here seven years ago," I said. My voice came out hoarse. I cleared my throat and forced out the rest of the words. "They killed her. The fae killed my mother."

CHAPTER 11

Ren

AARON'S EYES widened at my declaration. Marco squeezed my shoulder tighter, but I didn't want comfort right now. I wanted answers.

I pulled away from him, striding to the wall. One of the walls the fae had emerged from in my vision. I swiped my arm across my teary eyes and raised my voice in a ragged shout. "You! Fae! Where are you? Stop lurking around and come out of there. Own up to what you did, you fucking assholes. Don't you dare hide away and pretend you don't know—"

My voice cut off with a growl of frustration. I lashed out at the rock, my dragon's talons already protruding from my fingers. They gouged the wall, but I didn't get any satisfaction from that act of destruction. The fae hadn't emerged. Fucking cowards. More than a dozen of them ganging up on one woman, battering her until she couldn't even stand...

My jaw clenched. "Serenity," Aaron started, but I felt anything but serene. I whipped around, tossing off my jacket. If the fae wouldn't come to me, I'd just have to track them down and *make* them pay.

My muscles twanged as my body shifted fully into dragon form. I filled nearly half of the room. The pedestal suddenly looked tiny. I stalked around it, my nostrils flaring.

There. A faint scent remained under the cold rock smell. Like cut grass mixed with sleet. I'd never noticed that odor before, but every instinct in me told me it was the fae. I inhaled deeply, trying to follow the trail, and paused.

I could tell it was fae—and I could also tell it was old. Stale. My dragon senses suggested the scent had been left days ago. Maybe the fae woman who'd told us about the weasel and her companions had passed through here.

I let myself shrink back to near human size to dash through the narrow entryway. Then I prowled down the length of the cave back in dragon form. I tasted the air on my tongue, dragged more into my massive lungs.

Not a hint of fresh fae scent reached me. They were nowhere around. The bastards really had just left.

With a growl of frustration, I collapsed back into my human self. The stone floor chilled my bare skin, but I didn't care. I pulled my knees up to my chest and pressed my face to them, holding in a sob. Tears drew frigid streaks down my legs.

Mom was gone. She'd been gone for seven years, and

I'd known all that time she might be dead, but now it was completely real. There was no hoping for any other outcome.

I didn't want to accept it. She'd come here for me. Because she'd wanted to give me all the power she could, so I could take this role as leader of all shifter-kind. Because she hadn't wanted to put *me* in danger by bringing me with her. Maybe if we'd been together, if I'd known what I was then...

Footsteps scraped over the floor. One of the guys draped my jacket over my shoulders. They all gathered in a semi-circle around me.

"I knew we couldn't trust the fae," West muttered. "They helped the rogues, set us up every way they could."

"Quite the strategy," Marco said. "Make it look like we were taken down by our own kind so they couldn't get in trouble over breaking the treaty. Very sneaky. I'd almost admire their wiles if they hadn't been using them against me."

"I don't think this is the time for jokes," Nate said, with a frown I could hear.

Aaron knelt down in front of me. When I raised my head to meet my mate's eyes, he rested his hand over mine. His expression was solemn. "We won't let this stand," he said. "The fae committed a crime, and they'll answer for it."

"How?" I asked in a croak. My throat felt thick with unshed tears.

"When we come down from the mountain, the first thing we'd have done anyway is visit the centers of the shifter community to spread the word that you've been found and taken on your role as dragon shifter. We can start with the avian estate, since it's the closest to here and our mate-bond is already consummated—and because the monarch of the fae has her domain only a short distance away. We'll bring the matter straight to her."

"Isn't there something else we need to talk about first?" Marco said. "What happened with that crystal? Your mom came all the way up here for a reason, princess —what's this power she wanted you to have?"

I reached my awareness through the ache of grief inside me and the soreness of my overworked muscles. Nothing inside me felt all that different. *The flame of truth,* that strange figure had called it when I'd smashed the crystal. *Burn to destroy or burn away lies.*

My lungs tickled at the thought of breathing fire. Could I produce a different kind of flame now? I didn't think I could even manage to shift back into my dragon form after two transformations in such close succession. My endurance still had a ways to go.

"I'm not totally sure," I said. "It has something to do with my dragon fire and with finding the truth. The flame inside the crystal is what showed me what happened to my mother. Somehow I'm supposed to be able to use it to get at what is real? But it didn't come with an instruction manual or anything."

Wouldn't it have been nice if it had. I guessed, like everything else since my life had taken this crazy turn, I'd just have to figure it out as I went along.

"That sounds useful, given how things have been going," Nate said. "You'll be able to tell who to trust."

"Once I figure out how to use it." I gave my eyes another swipe and pushed myself onto my feet. My loss still weighed heavy on me, but I had my four alphas to protect now, even as they protected me. I had a whole community of shifters to look after.

And the fae who'd killed my mother were still out there, committing who knew what other crimes against us.

"All right," I said. "Let's get off this mountain, and then I want a meeting with the fae monarch."

I lifted my head at the smell of salt seeping into the SUV. We were coming up on the coast. Which meant coming up on the estate by the Pacific Ocean where Aaron oversaw the avian kin-group.

Today I was going to *meet* that kin-group as his mate and one of their leaders. My skin itched at the thought. I curled tighter into the back seat and looked at my phone again. Kylie had just replied to my last text.

I wish I could be there with you, Ren. You shouldn't have to deal with news like that without your bestie. I know how much your mom meant to you.

I wish you were here too, I wrote back. The one comfort of getting off the mountain had been getting my cell phone service back. Although there was still a lot I wasn't sure how to tell Kylie. It was easier to go back to joking around. *You're just sad you're missing out on all the eye candy.*

Hey, they're your mates! I don't mess around with taken guys. But you can't blame a girl for enjoying the view. She added a winking emoji. *Are you handling it okay? Is there anything you want me to send from here?*

I considered, but we'd only just moved into our apartment. I hadn't exactly accumulated a lot of possessions during my years living on the streets. Part of me longed to snuggle up under the crocheted blanket we'd spread on the back of the used couch we'd scored and feel that familiarity of home again. But I had other things to take care of first.

It wasn't just the avian estate up ahead. The fae monarch's domain lay nearby too.

I hadn't told Kylie about that part of this trip. Hadn't even told her what I'd seen of my mom's death, only that I'd seen it. If she knew I was about to go confront a bunch of murdering magical beings, she'd *really* freak out.

What was the point in worrying her when she was too far away to help?

"Are we there yet?" Marco called from the seat ahead of me with a mock-childish voice. I gently kicked the seatback, and he shot an amused smile my way.

Aaron chuckled where he was sitting at the front in his usual spot as navigator. "Almost. Why are cats always so restless?"

"Because we know we have so much to contribute to the world, and can't stand to be held back," Marco declared. He propped his feet against the driver's seat in front of him.

Nate, who was sitting in that seat, made a gruff sound of dismissal. "I don't remember you contributing a whole lot to *this* trip, other than picking out the most expensive dishes at the restaurant last night."

Marco waved him off. "I just spent a week on a mountain eating non-perishables. Including food that was outright poisoned. We *all* deserved a good meal after that."

No one looked at me as he said that, but I felt the shift in attention all the same. All of the guys except West had offered to keep me company in the back seat, but I'd told them I wanted a little time to myself to think and chat with Kylie. I knew they were still worried about my reaction to finding out about Mom's death. I hadn't wanted to eat a whole lot in the restaurant, true. I just wanted to get out here and see some justice done.

As if he'd picked up on that thought, Aaron directed his voice toward me. "As soon as we arrive, I'll send one of my people to arrange an audience with the fae monarch. It shouldn't take long for her to respond."

"And I'm sure they'll be so happy to entertain us," West grumbled where he was sitting beside Marco.

I ignored him. "Thank you," I said to Aaron.

The salt smell in the air thickened. The SUV pulled up to a wrought-iron gate set in a high stone wall. My pulse kicked up a notch. Instinctively, I slipped my hand into my pocket to squeeze Mom's locket. The solid metal made me feel slightly more grounded.

I think I'd better say my good-byes for the moment, I texted to Kylie. *It looks like I'm just about there.*

Go be the best dragon shifter queen they've ever seen!
she replied.

I smiled, but as I put away my phone, I didn't feel at
all queenly. I was wearing a tee and jeans and no make-
up, my body was still sore from all that hiking up and
down the mountain. I had no idea what to even expect
from a shifter estate.

Aaron had explained that the kin-groups each had a
sort of center of operations, the avians in the northwest,
the canines in the northeast, the felines in the southeast,
and the assorted group Nate ruled over in the southwest.
The alphas traveled throughout the country as they
needed to, but they met with their advisors and kept their
records on the estate. Any shifter who needed help could
always show up there and know they'd be taken care of.

The dragon shifters had an estate too—one that had
been left vacant for sixteen years. Right smack in the
middle of the country, so it didn't favor any of the kin
groups over the others. That was where my entire family
had been when the rogues had launched their first attack.

My gut twisted at the thought of going back to that
place. I had happy childhood memories from my first five
years, growing up there... but my last memories of the
house and the grounds around it were full of violence
and panic.

Trills of music filtered through the sides of the van. I
peered out the window. A huge mansion had just come
into view up ahead. All its windows shone with inner
light amid the deepening evening. White marble columns
framed the double doors, and sculptures of bird-like
figures clustered along the eaves of the angled roof.

The trees lining the drive leading up to the mansion were strung with sparkling lanterns. A massive courtyard lay between the forested grounds and the mansion's broad front steps. In that courtyard, a swarm of figures had gathered. They were whirling in time with the music, swinging lights of their own.

Then someone must have caught sight of the SUV. A cheer rose up. The dancers stilled to watch our arrival.

Aaron glanced back at me. "My kin are all looking forward to meeting you," he said. "They wanted to make your first visit here special."

I hugged myself, trying to contain my nerves. These shifters wanted to like me. I was their alpha's mate. But stepping out into this excited crowd was a far cry from being questioned and pawed over by a small group of villagers in the shifter town we'd stopped at on our way to the mountain. There had to be hundreds of people gathered together before us.

"I don't know what to say to them," I said. "Or what to do. Or—"

"Just be yourself. Be our Princess of Flames." Marco aimed his sly grin at me. "No one could ask for anything more than that."

I wasn't so sure about that. But as Nate drew the SUV to a stop at the edge of the courtyard, I pulled my back up straight.

This was it. This was the start of the whole rest of my life, as the dragon shifter who held the four shifter kin groups together. I'd fought to be here. And now I was going to damn well make as much of it as I could.

CHAPTER 12

West

A WOMAN who smelled like a sparrow bumped into me from behind. A second later, a sparrow shifter jostled me to the side with his elbow. Gritting my teeth, I wove toward the edge of the courtyard. Music seemed to be clanging from every direction, only slightly louder than the cacophony of voices. And there were a lot of voices. Avians always had an awful lot to say.

Wolves were pack animals, sure, but a proper pack was ten, maybe fifteen strong. We didn't enjoy *crowds*. No room to run, no room to maneuver. How anyone enjoyed them, I didn't have a clue. And no one here gave any deference to my status as alpha. All their attention was focused on *their* returning leader—and, of course, the mate at his side.

I glanced back over the bobbing heads. Aaron's kin had set up a platform in the middle of the courtyard so that he could stand there and show off Ren. The dragon shifter was smiling and shaking hands and accepting hugs, but her stance was just as uncertain as it'd been in that canine village when she'd been swarmed.

A twinge I didn't like ran through my chest. The impulse to go to her, to lend my presence as support. Was she really ready for this?

I set my jaw. If she wanted this role, she was going to have to be ready. This time I couldn't step in and usher her away to give her some breathing room. This was the eagle shifter's show. Anyway, she'd asked for this by consummating the mate-bond with Aaron. Let her have it.

I wrenched my eyes away and spotted Marco at the edge of the courtyard. I'd have expected the jaguar shifter to be right there in the middle of the festivities, given the way he usually chased after fun as if it were a particularly tasty mouse. But maybe he was having a private party of his own here. He'd gathered a group of shifters around him who didn't look at all avian. As I came up to them, I got a good whiff. Felines, all of them.

"What's with the cat convention over here?" I asked.

Marco's gaze slid to me. He flicked his fingers dismissively. "A kin delegation caught up with me here. The vampires back in New York are throwing a bit of a tantrum. Nothing we can't sort out by ourselves."

Vamps. I grimaced. "After that encounter on their territory, I can't blame them for being pissed off."

"Well, we didn't have much choice in tangling with them, did we? And now we get to tangle with the fae. Although to be fair, in that case the fae started it."

One of the other feline shifters tapped Marco's elbow. Marco leaned in to hear whatever comment the guy didn't want me listening in on. As if I were all that interested in their private chat. I was happy to leave the vamp-taming to them.

Of course, I'd rather be dealing with vamps than the fae. A prickle crept over my skin as I turned away.

Ren was so set on taking the fight to the monarch. She had no idea what she was getting into. No idea how fucking dangerous the fae could be. They'd killed her mother to stop her from getting to the mysterious power Ren now carried—which meant they'd see Ren as twice as much of a threat. Going to them, no matter how horrendous their past crimes were, was only asking for trouble.

But our dragon shifter didn't like hearing the word "no," did she? My eyes were drawn to her again where she stood on the platform. I couldn't deny that even in her plain human clothes there was something regal about her. Something majestic she was growing into.

Something I wanted to touch and taste and own.

A rush of desire flowed through my veins. I clamped down on it, pushing it away.

How could I know that feeling was really mine and not just a symptom of the mate-bond, which only existed because of what we were, not who we were? Every instinct was pushing me toward her, but that didn't mean it was the right decision. She had much more to learn—so much more discipline to develop...

I just had to stop myself from giving into the urge to be the one to teach her.

My people were counting on me to make the right choice here. To lead them in whatever direction would serve *them* best. Ren was getting the chance to show who she was as a shifter now. As the dragon shifter all these people had been waiting for. It wouldn't take much time to see if she'd shine or sputter out.

My gaze was still glued to her. Damn if she wasn't shining right now. She beamed at a woman who'd come up to the platform to pay her respects, and her face turned toward me. I ducked my head before she could catch me watching her.

She'd already seen far too much of the power she held over *me*. I had to keep my distance until I was sure.

~

Ren

Aaron touched the small of my back and leaned in so I could hear him over the noise of the crowd around us. "Doing okay?" he asked.

"Yeah," I said, with a smile I meant. My body swayed automatically to the music pealing out across the courtyard. The nervous energy I'd felt earlier had transformed into a more enjoyable exhilaration. "Doing good. I mean, it's a little overwhelming, but... Everyone's so nice. What could I complain about?"

He chuckled. "Glad to hear it. They've been waiting for this day for a long time."

And so had he. A little flare of pride sparked inside me. He'd led his people for so many years on his own, from when he was little more than a boy. And now I got to stand beside him.

I curled my fingers into the front of his shirt and pressed my lips to his. Aaron traced his thumb over my cheek, kissing me back gently but thoroughly, until I'd lost my breath. A jolt of desire shot through me. Suddenly I did mind the crowd around us quite a bit.

But they didn't mind our PDA. A cheer rose up around us. I pulled back, flushed and grinning. "Sorry."

Aaron outright laughed at my apology. "For what? They loved that." His smile turned roguish. "And so did I. Shifters aren't shy about showing affection any more than we're worried about showing our bodies. Look around."

He nodded to the crowd. I let my gaze travel over the mass of bodies around our little platform. The crowd stretched all across the massive courtyard to the ring of marble arches at its border and the stretch of trees beyond. Despite the lanterns scattered around the place, it was getting pretty dark. I hadn't noticed the behavior he was talking about until I peered harder.

Oh. All across the fringes of the courtyard, pressed up against the columns of the arches or right in the midst of their fellow revelers, couples were going at it. Kissing, heavy petting, the works. I saw one young couple who looked ready to seal the deal right there on a stone bench between two of the arches. A woman lolled her head in bliss as her partner stroked her breasts beneath her shirt. A group of three were taking turns devouring each other's mouths. Apparently dragon shifters weren't the only ones who enjoyed multiple mates.

The flush on my face trickled right down my body. "Wow. Okay, I guess if I should worry about anything, it's that your kin are going to think I'm a prude."

Aaron looped his arm around my waist. "You *shouldn't* worry about anything. They'll take you exactly as you are. And those activities might be a little more, er, extreme tonight than is usual in public even for us. People have a lot of time to make up for."

It took me a second to realize what he was talking about. West had told me that none of the shifter kin could have children while their alpha went un-mated. Now it was no holds barred in the baby-making department. I guessed there'd be an awful lot of new avians being born nine months from now.

An awful lot of all sorts of shifter babies, once I fully accepted all of my mates.

The thought gave me a strange twinge: giddy excitement and anxious uncertainty mixed together. I shouldn't be neglecting the other guys, even now—I wouldn't ignore Aaron when we were at the other kin-group estates, after all.

I searched the crowd again, this time looking for the rest of my mates. I didn't spot Nate or West, although my innate sense of their presence told me they were nearby. Marco was standing near one of the arches, talking with a few other shifters.

And frowning, which was not an expression I saw on his face often. My stomach twisted. Was something wrong?

"Hey," I said to Aaron. "Is it all right if I circulate

around a little, or am I supposed to stay up here the whole time?"

"Go right ahead," he said. "The estate should be completely safe. I have people checking everyone who's arrived for their kin sign."

I hopped off the platform and was immediately swept up in the bustle of the celebration. Aaron's kin grasped my arms with friendly squeezes, shouted joyful comments into my ears, and beamed at me as if... well, as if they'd been waiting sixteen years just to meet me. I smiled back until my face ached with it. My heart thumped fast, but I didn't want to leave this chaos yet.

This was the first time I'd been somewhere I completely belonged since I'd fled with my mother all those years ago.

I gradually wove through the crowd toward the arch where I'd seen Marco. When I reached it, at first I thought he was gone. Then I heard his voice carrying from the other side of the thick marble column.

"I don't see how that's any of your business."

"None of our business?" a guy retorted. "We're your kin. And the security of our kin-group depends on you getting off your ass and locking her in."

Locking her in. What were they talking about? I hesitated, suspecting that if I walked right into that conversation, it'd stop in an instant.

"I'm working on it," Marco said. "I'm sure it was a hell of a lot easier for the alphas whose mates knew what they were getting into more than a couple weeks in advance."

Someone else, this one a woman, snorted. "Where are

those charms you always speak so highly of? You know how many there are who'd happily take your place if it looks like there's an opening. And until you've consummated that bond—"

"I *know*," Marco snapped. "Thank you so much for your concern, but I assure you I'll get the job done. And before wolf boy or our resident grizzly gets in there too."

His tone was so callous my hackles rose. I backed up, merging back with the crowd, suddenly hating the thought of any of them noticing I was there.

It was me they were talking about, obviously. They were hassling Marco about our uncertain bond. But he hadn't exactly defending me, had he? He'd made it sound as if... as if being my mate was some kind of competition. Or a *job*. That word he'd actually used.

My mind darted back to the way he'd talked to me the other night when we almost had consummated our relationship. He'd gone on about how much he cared about me, about the life we'd have together...

My stomach turned. Had he really meant any of that? Or had he just thought a bunch of sweet nothings was the best way to get me to give in to his "charms"?

More avian shifters greeted me, and I managed to smile, but a sliver of pain jabbed at my gut. I'd assumed if I could trust *any*one, it was my mates. Even West, despite his gruffness. What if I'd been wrong?

Without meaning to, I wandered back into the vicinity of the platform. Aaron hopped down to meet me. He took in my expression and brought his hand to the side of my face. I leaned into his touch, taking as much comfort from it as I could.

"Is the celebration getting to be a bit much?" he said.

No. I wasn't going to let some stupid remarks stop me from making the most of this moment. I could decide how to deal with Marco later, when I could speak to him alone. Tonight was about celebrating what we'd gained.

I wrapped my fingers around Aaron's palm. "I'm fine. Want to dance?"

"I'll never turn down that request from you." He set his other hand on my waist and twirled me around, fast enough that a laugh jolted out of me despite myself. Then he pulled me close to him, both of us turning together with the melody spilling through the air.

"How soon can you reach out to the fae monarch?" I asked. I couldn't forget that reason for coming here either. I wasn't going to be able to feel right until I'd gotten some sort of justice for Mom.

"I already have," Aaron said. "I sent one of my people to her citadel about an hour ago. We should hear the answer by tomorrow." He squeezed my hand tighter. "And if she tries to refuse to hear us, believe me, I'll make sure she changes her tune."

CHAPTER 13

Ren

THE SKY HAD DEEPENED to near-black over the garden, twinkling with a dusting of stars. I tipped my head to them, letting their faint light soak into me, as I meandered down the path.

The avian kin celebration was only just starting to wind down. Music and chatter still carried over the hedges from the courtyard. I'd finally slipped away through one of the arches into this quieter space a few minutes ago. Sometimes a girl needed room to breathe.

The warm, salty air was such a relief after all that time in the mountain's cold. I closed my eyes, drinking it in. A faint breeze rustled through the flowers and hedges around me. A sweet perfume rose up from the blossoms to mingle with the ocean scent. The crash of the waves sounded from the other side of the house, just barely audible to my shifter ears.

As I breathed in again, another scent reached my nose. Something darker, earthier with a prickle of pine. I knew before I opened my eyes that I'd see West nearby.

The wolf shifter was standing by a wooden latticework. A flowering vine climbed across the interlaced slats over a stone bench like the ones around the courtyard. West was facing away from me, toward the far end of the garden and the top of the estate wall visible beyond it. His hands were slung in the pockets of his jeans, and his head was tipped to the side at a thoughtful angle.

I hesitated, the mate-bond urging me to go to him while what was probably common sense suggested I leave him be. If he'd wanted company, he wouldn't be all the way over here while the party was still happening. And it wasn't as if he'd ever acted all that excited to spend time with *me*.

But maybe that was exactly why I should go to him. He was a jerk to me some of the time—okay, a lot of the time—but I could understand why. I'd seen how much he cared about his kin. The shifters' dependence on the ties between dragon shifter and alphas *had* gone terribly wrong after my mother's disappearance.

He felt the same draw I did. Maybe being a jerk was the only way he knew how to fend that desire off while he made his decision.

He should know that I wanted to give him a chance, at least. That I would do everything I could for his kin as well as Aaron's and the other guys' if he met me halfway. If he decided to forsake the mate-bond and look to form a new one separate from tradition, it wasn't going to be because *I* pushed him away.

And maybe a little part of me was remembering that one kiss he'd given me, after the rogues' first ambush. The passion in it that had left my head spinning. And the way he'd looked at me the other night in the tent...

My skin flushed a little just at the memory.

I ambled around a clump of red and pink rose bushes and a magnolia tree. I wasn't trying to be quiet, and West could probably smell my presence just as well as I'd smelled his, but it still startled me a little when he spoke.

"Did being the center of attention get a little old, Sparks?" he said without turning around.

I rolled my eyes at his back, even though he couldn't see my expression. "I spent most of my life practicing *not* drawing attention. I think it'll be a while before stuff like this feels totally comfortable."

He made a non-committal sound. Well, he hadn't told me to take off. That was some kind of progress.

I walked up beside him, peering in the same direction he was looking. "Don't you trust Aaron's sentries to keep a close enough eye on things?"

"You can't be careful enough with the fae," West said. "I heard he's already sent someone to request the parlay. She has to know you're here, and where we were before now. She'll know what the request is about."

"Do you think she already knows some of her people killed my mother? Do you think it was her *idea*?" My chest tightened. If the ruler of the fae had ordered the murder of the ruler of the shifters... That would be an act of all-out war, wouldn't it? Why would they hate us enough to do that?

"It's unlikely," West admitted, to my relief. "The last thing the fae are is stupid. But the monarch will have set the tone of conversation that made her underlings think it was a good idea. And I have trouble believing seven years could have gone by without word getting back to her. But she's stayed quiet. No interest in filling us in."

"What will happen if they decide they want to start some kind of war?" I asked. The image of the fae blasting Mom with their magic flashed through my mind. I shivered. "Can we really fight back?"

West's mouth curled into a grim smile. "Shifters are strong. It takes at least a few fae to tackle just one of us, weaklings like that weasel rogue aside. And there are a lot more of us than there are of them. We'd give them a good fight. But that doesn't mean we should be begging for one."

"I don't *want* to fight," I said. "I just want some answers. I want the fae who killed my mom to face some kind of consequences. I don't think that's asking a lot."

"You don't know the fae," West said.

In the pale moonlight, his handsome face looked suddenly haunted. Maybe I didn't know the fae yet, but it was clear he did. The pain I could sense echoing through him made my own heart squeeze. I swallowed thickly.

"What did they do to you?"

His gaze jerked toward me for the first time, his penetrating green eyes meeting mine. "What makes you think they did anything?"

I raised my eyebrows. "Other than the fact that it's

written all over your face and in your voice? I'm a newbie shifter, not an idiot."

He turned, bringing his lean body that much closer to mine. Close enough that a rush of heat washed through me from head to toe. He cocked his head with an expression I couldn't quite read, somewhere between curiosity and anguish and defiance. His voice dropped, the clear throaty tone tingling into my ears.

"Do you really care? Or do you just think you should?"

I stared back at him. It had suddenly gotten very hard to think over the clang of desire ringing through my body. Thankfully that wasn't a very hard question to answer.

"I care. Of course I care. Do *you* really think I'd put up with half the shit-talking you do if I couldn't see there's a hell of a lot more to you than that—more that I want to know?"

"What makes you think the rest will be any different from what you've already seen, Sparks?"

My own voice dipped lower to match his, with a slightly teasing edge. "I don't know. But I've heard dragon shifters tend to be extra perceptive about these sorts of things. And by the way, I'm actually starting to like that nickname, so if the point of it is to annoy me, you'll have to find a new one."

"I'll give that some thought," he said with a twitch of his mouth. I couldn't tell if he'd suppressed a frown or a smile. I was too busy being distracted by how close his mouth was to mine. Not much more than a foot of space between us. Practically nothing at all. And then some genius part of my brain came up with the perfect excuse to touch him.

"That scar you've got. The one that almost *glows*. Is that from fighting with the fae?" I reached for his chest, holding my breath as I did.

West caught my hand an inch from grazing his pecs. His fingers closed around mine, firm and hot. There was so much heat radiating off him that for a second I thought I might melt.

"Are you sure that's what you want to do?" he said, so dark and low it was almost a whisper.

An ache had formed between my legs. I wet my lips. Fuck it. "No," I said. "I want *this*."

I tangled my other hand in his silvery auburn hair and pressed my mouth to his.

A groan reverberated from West's chest. He kissed me back hard, letting go of my hand to grip my waist and pull me flush against him. The heat of his body enveloped me, as if we weren't two people but two parts of one whole. Two parts desperate to meld back together.

I clutched his shirt, losing myself in the crush of his mouth and the demanding slide of his tongue. There was nothing I could imagine wanting more than this.

My hips arched against West's of their own accord. With a hungry growl, he lifted me off my feet and laid me on the stone bench without breaking the kiss. He braced himself over me, his body grazing mine tantalizingly. I whimpered and tugged him closer. The bulge in his jeans brushed my sex, and I rocked against him. He let out another groan and dropped his head to devour my neck with the hot slide of his tongue.

I gasped, groping him with an abandon that would have embarrassed me if he hadn't seemed just as frantic for release. My fingers found the hem of his shirt and trailed up under it over his bare back.

West grasped my hips, shifting them so his erection could hit my clit at an even better angle through our clothes. A moan slipped from my lips.

I didn't care that some other revelers might wander into the garden and see us, hear us. He was *mine* and I was his, and we were meant for this. From the moment I'd been born; from the moment he'd been named alpha. Before all the violence and the bitterness had wrenched us apart.

"Westley," I murmured, ducking my head to try to reclaim his mouth.

At the sound of his full name, West stiffened. He pushed off me so suddenly that for a few seconds all I could do was lie there blinking up at him, my body throbbing at the loss of contact.

He stared back at me. A tremble ran through him. His hands clenched at his sides. His mouth was still red from kissing me and his cock still hard against the fly of his jeans, but his eyes had gone abruptly cold.

"No," he said. "I'm not *Westley* to you, and don't pretend that I am."

I sat up, my breath coming in a rasp. What was he talking about? "I didn't mean anything— One of the shifters in your village called you that, and I remembered, and it just seemed..."

It had seemed natural, in the moment. But obviously

not to him. I didn't know how to explain it. I'd just been following my instincts.

"You've been gone for sixteen years," he said flatly. "You don't know me, and I don't owe you anything. I don't *need* anything from you. I've held my position as alpha all that time, and I'll damn well keep being alpha whether I accept your terms or not."

"West," I started, but his expression shuttered even more. My voice faltered.

He stalked off, striding down the garden paths toward the courtyard. I gazed after him, feeling achingly horny and alone—and more bewildered than I liked to admit.

CHAPTER 14

Ren

AFTER THE FESTIVITIES had carried on far into the night, I'd been escorted to rooms reserved for the dragon shifter. It was a relief to roll out of the elegant oak sleigh bed the next morning and amble into a private dining area where I didn't have to face even one more stranger. The wide, white-walled room was tucked away between the estate's dragon shifter quarters and those assigned to the alphas, and no one else got to use it.

When I slipped inside, Nate was already digging into a breakfast of poached eggs, bacon, toast, and fresh-cut fruit at the polished teak table. The mingling sweet and savory smells set my mouth watering. Aaron was standing by the broad window that overlooked the ocean, a cup of coffee nestled in his hands. He turned from the view of the crashing waves and smiled in greeting.

"Did you sleep all right, Serenity?"

"Looks like I've missed half the morning already, so I'd say yeah." I ambled over to the buffet where the spread of platters was laid out. Man, where to start? My stomach gurgled eagerly. "It's a nice place you've got here."

Aaron laughed. "I can't really take much credit for that. The estate has been passed from alpha to alpha for as long as anyone can remember. It's a nice perk to go with the responsibilities, though."

Nate patted the table beside him as I headed over with a heaping plate. "This side gives the best view of the ocean."

"Or are you just saying that to keep me close?" I teased.

To my relief, the bear shifter grinned. Things had felt a little awkward between us since I'd told him off for being over-protective, but I didn't want him to think I was holding some kind of grudge. And I sure hoped he wasn't either. The vibe I got from him as I sat down in the next chair was a little hesitant but warm.

"I can't say that isn't an extra benefit," he said. I let my leg rest next to his under the table, and his grin grew.

I wanted him to remember what I'd told him about how to treat me, but I still *wanted* him, too. He ran his hand over my thigh to squeeze my knee in a gesture that would have seemed playful if it hadn't also sent a bolt of desire to my core. Oh, I wanted him all right, and I had no doubt he felt the same way.

But Aaron's comment about the alpha line of succession stirred up thoughts of last night. Of the deeper awkwardness I'd felt with my other alphas. First there'd been that weird conversation I'd overheard between Marco and his kin. And then the interlude with West that had somehow gone completely wrong. I still didn't know exactly what he'd been so upset about. But that comment he'd made had stuck with me, especially after the stuff with Marco.

I'll damn well keep being alpha whether I accept your terms or not.

Aaron had talked before about having to fight to keep his position as alpha. More than once, other avian shifters who'd wanted a shot at the leadership had challenged him. I'd been too occupied with my mother's mystery to think much about how my reappearance would change the dynamics of ruling for all the guys.

I dipped the corner of my toast into the perfectly runny egg yolk and took a bite, but now my mind was churning. I couldn't turn it off. Why should I? *I* was supposed to be ruling the shifters too. I should understand the ins and outs of every aspect as well as I could.

Aaron came over to sit down across from me. I glanced at him. "Is it going to be easier for you to be... respected as the alpha now that I'm here? And we're officially mated? I mean, like, fewer people challenging you or whatever?"

He nodded, considering me with his bright blue eyes. "A lot of the turmoil in the shifter community has come down to not having a dragon shifter around to provide the usual balance. With people seeing that you're here and taking on that role, they'll be less restless." His tone turned wry. "And there are many who'll feel your accepting me is an additional mark in my favor."

"And that'll go for all of the kin-groups, I guess."

Nate raised his head, his expression concerned. "You don't need to worry about that, Ren. You're here. You're with us as much as you're comfortable being. No one should be rushing you. We can handle any challenges that can come our way."

Except Marco kind of had been rushing me, hadn't he? Even though he'd tried to tell me he wasn't. I speared a piece of bacon but didn't lift it from my plate.

"I know," I said. I didn't want to outright accuse the jaguar shifter of something to the other guys. How could I put it? "I heard Marco talking with some feline kin yesterday. It sounded like there are a lot of them who are restless. I was just wondering if he's had more trouble than the rest of you?"

Nate made a humming sound. "Cat temperaments don't do well with being ruled over in general. They're always squabbling."

"On top of that, I'd imagine Marco being the youngest of us didn't help," Aaron said. "He was only ten years old when the previous feline alpha died. And you've probably noticed his personality can be a little... provocative."

"He likes to run off his mouth," Nate muttered. "Everything's a big joke."

Aaron chuckled. "I think he cares more than he likes to show. But yes, that's what I meant."

Marco cared a lot about staying alpha, anyway. I

chewed and swallowed, but the bacon had lost its taste. My stomach had gone tight.

"But Marco's handled himself all this time," Nate said, giving my knee another quick squeeze. "You don't need to worry about him either."

Before I could decide whether I wanted to say anything else about that, there was a knock on the door. "News from the fae, sir," a voice called in.

Aaron straightened up. "Come in," he said. "Whatever it is, everyone here can hear it."

A tall, gawky young man who brought to mind a heron came into the room. He gave his alpha a quick bob of a bow. "The monarch has granted your request of a parlay," he said. "She is willing to meet with you and your party tomorrow at noon on the neutral ground."

"Did she say anything else?" Aaron asked.

The heron shifter shook his head. "She didn't look surprised to be asked, though."

Because she'd already been expecting us, like West had suggested? My stomach knotted even more. My fingers curled around the fork with the sudden impulse to pocket the silverware, as if that would make the situation more under my control. I hadn't quite shaken my thieving past yet.

As the messenger ducked out, I turned back to Aaron. "Is that what you expected?"

"Delaying by a day isn't a surprise," he said. "She wouldn't want to seem overly accommodating. Other than that, it's pretty hard to read the fae on the best of days. I don't see any warning signs." His gaze turned more thoughtful. "Our wolf alpha has been making you nervous."

"He really doesn't trust the fae. I'd call it paranoia if I didn't get the feeling he's got a good reason to. Where is West, anyway?" I figured Marco was sleeping in like usual, but getting a late start wasn't like West.

Nate motioned to the window. "He was stalking out of here when I came in. He's probably patrolling the grounds right now."

Aaron shrugged. "If that's what makes him feel more at ease. The fae *are* difficult to deal with. But you'll have all of us with you to support you, Serenity."

With every time he said it, I got more used to hearing my full name used. It reminded me how much more I was than the teen living on the streets who'd had to resort to stealing to get by. I'd found a real place for myself here. And just like the alphas had with their positions, I was going to hold onto mine with everything I had in me.

I really wasn't feeling all that hungry anymore though. I forced down a few more bites of toast and stood up. "Is there anything I should know about that's planned for today? Or can I just explore?"

"Stay within the estate, unless one of us is with you," Aaron said. "There's a formal dinner arranged for tonight where you'll get to meet representatives from many of the powerful avian families. Until then, enjoy yourself however you'd like. I have a few admin-type concerns to take care of now that I'm back, but I'll look for you later."

The warmth in his gaze made me think of all the ways I'd enjoyed myself with him. I'd been too exhausted last night to think of using my bed for anything other than zonking out on. But there were so many other possibilities... The huge mattress was big enough that it could have held five of us easily.

"I look forward to that," I said with a twitch of my eyebrows. The warmth in his eyes went from gentle to smoldering in an instant. Oh yes, I was looking forward to it a lot.

I *was* also looking forward to taking in the rest of the estate. Last night I hadn't seen anything other than the courtyard and the garden, by darkness.

I slipped through my rooms and out into one of the mansion's main halls. The ocean breeze filled the whole place with that refreshingly salty smell and took the edge off the summer heat. The white washed walls, teak floors, and big windows all through the open concept space made me feel like I'd stepped into a massive—and exclusive—beach cottage. The perks of being alpha indeed.

I hadn't made it very far when Marco emerged into the hall up ahead of me. He gave me his usual sly smirk as he sauntered over.

"Good morning, princess."

I wanted to smile and say it back, to pretend nothing was wrong. But with his indigo eyes on me and all the questions that had been whirling in my head, I froze up. The jaguar shifter cocked his head at my hesitation. "Is everything all right, Ren?"

This wasn't the best place for a confrontation. But at the moment there was no one else in sight. And I didn't really want to go somewhere private with him, not until I had a few answers. I braced myself and raised my chin.

"I don't know," I said. "It seemed like maybe things aren't totally all right with your kin? You didn't look very happy talking with them yesterday."

"Oh, that." Marco waved off my concern with a flick of his lithe hand. "A little vampire trouble, soon to be taken care of. The bloodsuckers just like making a fuss. I sent the delegation off to deal with it before they could get the avians' feathers too ruffled."

"Ah," I said. Well, of course he wasn't going to come right out and admit to the other things they'd talked about. I paused and then forced myself to keep going. "I've been thinking about some of the things you said the other night. About how much I mean to you. How much you want to start our lives together."

An eager light lit in Marco's eyes. He stepped closer, his voice dropping lower. "And where did those thoughts lead you next?"

Part of my body still responded to him the way it always had. My fingers itched to tangle in his dark hair, my lips to feel his against them. But another part of me, tight around my heart, balked at his eagerness. Because what was he *really* eager for?

I drew in a breath, keeping my gaze fixed on him. "I was wondering whether you actually meant any of it, or if the only reason being with me matters to you is so you can make a better claim as alpha."

Marco's jaw twitched. The light in his eyes went out. He managed a chuckle, but I didn't need any supernatural sensitivity to tell it sounded stiff. He summoned his familiar jaunty tone. "Princess, if someone's been telling you stories—"

And here he was, still fucking lying to me. My temper flared, fueled by a burn of betrayal spreading through my chest. "I heard it straight from your mouth last night," I snapped. "Talking about me like I'm a job you need to finish, a prize you're going to grab before the others. So don't pretend you have no idea what I'm talking about."

For once, Marco seemed to have nothing at all to say. His lips parted and just stayed that way as he stared at me. I could read the panic and guilt in him as clearly as if it'd been written in capital letters on his face.

I clenched my teeth against the pain swelling inside me. So it was all true. He couldn't even start to explain himself.

"I'm not a cat toy," I said, "so forget about treating me like one."

Then I turned and hurried off in the opposite direction before my tears caught up with me.

CHAPTER 15

Aaron

THE LAST ROOM I took Serenity into was the library. She sucked in her breath as she took in the bookshelves built into every wall from floor to ceiling, the clusters of sofas and armchairs on the deep-pile rug, and the view of the ocean from the two tall windows.

I smiled with a rush of pride. I might not be able to take full credit for this house, but I'd taken care to make it as welcoming as possible.

"And let me guess," my dragon shifter said, gesturing to the packed shelves. "You've read every one of those."

I laughed. "Hardly. But I did spend a lot of time in here when I was growing into my role, in between meetings with my advisors. I didn't have a senior alpha to guide me directly, so I found as much direction as I could in the books the previous alphas have accumulated over the decades."

"I used to read a lot, when my mom was still around," she said. "The library was an easy place to get out of the apartment for a while, where no one would bother you if you found a quiet little nook for yourself. But once she left, and I ended up on the street..."

A shadow crossed her face. I wished I could brush it away with a caress of my hand. She didn't like to talk much about those years after her mother had disappeared, but every time she mentioned them, she couldn't hide how deeply the experience had wounded her.

But she was healing on her own. With every strength she discovered in herself, with every bit she let us in, she was coming back to the woman she was meant to be.

"You can find a quiet little nook in here whenever you want," I said. "The house is yours as much as it's mine."

She ducked her head for a second, as if embarrassed. Then she smiled at me with the glow of confidence that was coming to her more and more often now. The rush of pride that filled my chest now was for her. Followed by the desire to show her exactly how much I adored her, in every possible way up against one of those shelves.

The clock on the fireplace mantle chimed. No time for that sort of diversion now. I took her hand, enjoying the way her slender fingers automatically closed around mine.

"We should go back to your rooms. You'll want to pick out a dress for the dinner. People will expect to see all of us a little decked out."

The corner of her mouth curled higher. "So a tee and

jeans isn't going to cut it, is what you're saying? All right, all right. I've got nothing against dresses. Let's make me into a real princess."

But as we strolled back to the dragon shifter's quarters hand in hand, another hint of shadow crossed her expression. Her fingers tightened slightly around mine. When she didn't speak, I glanced over at her. "Is something bothering you? You can tell me anything, you know."

"I know." She smiled again, but crookedly this time. "You don't have to worry—it's got nothing to do with you, or your amazing house. But it's not something I really want to talk about right now. If I feel like I do later, you'd be the first person I'll go to."

I couldn't ask for more than that. "Fair enough." I ushered her through her sitting room and into the vast bedroom that had belonged to generations of dragon shifters when they visited the avian estate. A private bath off to the side, a bed big enough for dragon shifter and four alphas, and several huge teak wardrobes. I walked up to one and tugged it open.

"The dragon shifter line tends to be pretty consistent in size," I said. "Some of the clothes in here might be a tad too small or too large, but we can always have a piece tailored if need be."

Serenity came up behind me. Her eyes widened. She fingered the drifts of silk and satin in their array of colors, a giggle escaping her. "I feel like a kid who just discovered the world's best dress-up box."

I chuckled. "Take your time. You should go out there tonight feeling every bit the princess."

I stepped back as she pawed through the dresses. She pulled out a few and tossed them onto the end of the bed for further consideration. "You said I'm going to meet some of the prominent avians," she said. "So there are shifter families with more power than others?"

"Like in any community," I said. "Sometimes it's based on the families of past alphas, sometimes just who fought best or contributed the most in past times of trouble... They don't have any official authority, but the rest of my kin would listen to them above others. So I try to keep them happy, as long as that doesn't mean making everyone else unhappy. You'll meet some of my family tonight too. My sister should be getting here in time for the dinner."

She glanced over at me as she shut the wardrobe, the last of her selections draped over her arm. "You have a sister?"

"Alice. Two years younger. Twice as fierce." I grinned. "She made herself my unofficial bodyguard when we were growing up. And she's done enough martial arts training to have earned that title. I think you two will get along well. And she'll watch out for you as much as she does me."

"Well, I'm looking forward to meeting her, at least." She strode over to the bed and threw the last dress on with the others. "Now let's get on with the decking out."

Ren

I ran my hands over the smooth fabric of the dresses, trying to lose myself in the moment. It was hard. The guilty expression on Marco's face had been nagging at me all day.

I'd trusted him. I thought I could, because he was my mate, because of the bond we shared, even if it wasn't fully consummated. But apparently he didn't feel it the same way I did. I was just a means to an end, not a person he cared about.

Aaron put his hands on my shoulders and rubbed them up and down. His touch brought me back to the present. He didn't ask again what was wrong, even though he could probably tell I was thinking about it again.

At least I had him. He cared about me. He believed in me. I could lean on him while I figured out where the hell things were going with the rest of my mates.

"You want to help?" I asked, letting a little heat creep into my voice.

Aaron raised his eyebrows, an answering spark lighting in his eyes. "Now that's an invitation I can't imagine turning down," he murmured.

I lifted my arms, and he tugged my T-shirt off me. His hands settled on my bare waist. He leaned over my shoulder, his breath tickling over my collarbone. "So, which one should we start with?"

My nipples had pebbled inside my bra. I squashed the urge to forget the dresses and just have him on me. Instead, I studied the ones I'd picked out.

Now that I was considering them together, the black

gown seemed overly stuffy. I didn't want to look like I thought I was attending a funeral. I picked up the silky lavender one that had caught my eye. "How about this?"

"I think it'll be lovely on you."

Aaron reached around to undo the button on my jeans. He tugged them down, and I stepped out of them. The tracing of his fingers over my skin left me a little breathless.

I eased up the dress over my body and waited as he zipped up the back. He came with me to the full-length mirror hanging on the wall between two of the wardrobes. The silver frame was almost as shiny as the glass.

I definitely didn't look like some girl off the streets now. That was a woman gazing back at me. The silk hugged my slim frame, rippling like water around my legs. The lavender did look lovely with my dark brown hair. But something about it didn't feel quite right.

I ambled back to the bed and shrugged that dress off. My hands fell on the gold one in the middle. The embroidered leaf pattern around the shoulders and bodice gave it a little more structure, and I liked the faint coordinating pattern marked into the satin fabric.

"Another excellent choice," Aaron said with a smile.

That dress had its zipper on the side, but he helped me with it anyway. As the fabric settled into place against my skin, a sense of certainty was already rising over me. I headed back to the mirror, the gown's small train whispering across the floor behind me.

My breath caught when I saw my reflection. The

gold fabric brought out the amber in my eyes, making them look like little flames. The cut hugged my hips slightly before flowing over my thighs, giving my figure a little more curve. I looked regal. Powerful.

I didn't just look like a princess. I looked like a *queen*. Woe betide anyone who messes with this dragon shifter.

My chin rose instinctively. Aaron's smile grew. "This one?" he said.

I didn't need to try any of the others. "This one," I agreed.

He pulled me closer to him. The press of his hands over the soft, smooth fabric felt amazing. And so did the press of his lips when he brought them to mine.

We kissed long and deep. My arms rose to loop behind his neck. He angled his head to kiss me harder, and I hummed encouragingly against his mouth. With a groan, he slid his hands up my sides to skim the curve of my breasts.

"You look fantastic with this on," he muttered. "But the only thing I want to do now is take it off you."

"I'm not really seeing any problem with that plan."

He grimaced against my cheek. "I'm supposed to meet with my advisors in a few minutes, to talk over the latest developments before the dinner starts. And to come up with a plan for our parlay tomorrow."

Our parlay with the fae monarch. My desire cooled at that thought. I stepped back to peer into his eyes. "How dangerous do you think it's going to be, meeting them face to face?"

He cupped my cheek, teasing his thumb over my temple in a reassuring caress. "They didn't outright attack us on the mountain. We can't trust them, but they're bound by the word they've given, the treaties they've agreed to uphold—in a magical sense. We just have to watch that they don't find some loophole like they did by using the rogues to their benefit. The entire shifter community will know we went to the neutral ground to talk with them. They can't hurt us without bringing an awful lot of pain on themselves."

He didn't sound overly worried. And with the fae monarch's domain right next door, he should know just how much trouble they were likely to stir up.

I dragged in a breath, not sure whether I was more nervous about meeting these bigwig shifters tonight or about meeting the fae tomorrow.

"You've got this," Aaron added. "And we'll be right there with you, just like always."

I nodded, suddenly too choked up on emotion to speak. He drew me to him again. This kiss felt softer and somehow more passionate at the same time. As if he were offering up all the devotion he felt in the brush of his lips against mine. I kissed him back hungrily, wanting that feeling. Needing it. Needing to give the same back to him.

Could I really call this love after just a couple weeks? I didn't know how else to describe the glow of happiness that filled me, being there in my eagle shifter's arms.

Aaron eased back, his eyes shining as if he'd heard what I hadn't let myself say out loud. "I really do have to go. But I'll see you soon at the dinner. Why don't you— There's a terrace overlooking the ocean just past our private dining room. If you'd like, you could take a walk out there. I've always found it calming. I'll send someone for you when it's time."

The way my nerves were jumping, a calming stroll sounded like just what I needed. "Thanks," I said. "I'll do that."

CHAPTER 16

Ren

THE SUN WAS JUST STARTING to come down over the ocean. It lit up the water with drifts of sparkles.

I walked across the stone tiles to the railing that surrounded the private terrace, drinking in the aquatic scents carried by the breeze. It was hard to stay anxious with that gorgeous scenery in front of me and the soothing crash of the waves filling my ears. I was a dragon shifter. The last dragon shifter in existence. Anyone who tried to mess with me was making the worst decision of their life.

My fingers curled around the cool marble surface of the railing. I raised my head high. The breeze rippled through my hair and through the flowing skirt of my dress. I felt the power of my heritage rippling through me too. And the little flame of power Mom had led me to, still flickering in the depths of my chest. Where was that going to lead me?

I had the sudden, wild urge to leap over the railing and down toward the beach. I could do it. The sandy slope below looked a little uneven, but nothing I couldn't manage a good tumble on.

But even as the urge rose up, I knew that jump wouldn't give me the same rush all my leaps and falls before used to. I'd experienced what it was like to *really* fly now. Nothing could compare to that.

Someday I'd be able to hold my dragon form for hours on end. Just soar and soar as far as my wings could take me. That sounded awfully nice right now.

I'd carried my purse out with me. My phone buzzed with a text alert. I pulled it out, already knowing it had to be Kylie. My best friend was the only one who had the number. There wasn't anyone else in my life I'd trusted enough to want to stay in contact with... except for the guys, now, and I hadn't needed to be apart from them yet.

What would it be like once we had to split up? They'd have alpha duties to take care of. Sometimes they'd need to be off at different estates, and I wouldn't be able to stay with all of them at once. Even with all the uncertainties whirling around us, part of me ached to keep them close.

All these crazy feelings had to get easier to deal with once I'd had more time to get used to the situation, right?

What's up in royal shifter land? Kylie had texted. I smiled and leaned back against the railing as I typed my reply.

Big fancy dinner upcoming. You would not believe the dress I've got on.

Ren in a dress!!! OMG, I can't believe I'm missing this. Take a pic. That's an order.

I laughed and held the phone out to try to capture as much of the dress as possible in a selfie. When I sent it to her, Kylie replied with a selfie of her face with her eyes wide in shock.

You look spectacular, Ren. Those four alphas of yours are going to have their hands full fighting off the rest of the guys there.

I don't think people are coming to this dinner looking to hook up, I wrote back. *It sounds like there's a lot of Serious Political Business to discuss. Heads of major shifter families and stuff. I guess they want to make sure I'm really real and that Aaron didn't just make up that they finally found me?*

So you're that big a deal, huh?

Yeah. I paused, thinking about my conversation with Marco this morning with a twist in my gut. *It seems like having a dragon shifter around as their mate makes it a lot easier for the other shifters to accept them as alphas. I guess that's what they meant about me uniting all the kin-groups. Seems like a lot of responsibility.*

But they'll help you through it. You can handle it. You don't think you're still in danger, do you? Now that you took care of those rogue douchebags?

My gut twisted harder. I didn't want to tell her about that continuing threat—or about how wary I was of the meeting with the fae monarch tomorrow. *Not immediately, it doesn't seem like. I don't know what to* expect going forward. I'm still getting used to BEING a shifter. There's been a lot of conflict in the kin-groups since my mom disappeared, I guess, and I don't know the half of it yet.

Well, you look after yourself. It doesn't matter what they want from you. You've got to put yourself first. And if anyone argues with that, you send them to me and I'll set them straight.

I had to smile at that. I'd bet she would too. Kylie always had my back—even with all this supernatural chaos descending on us.

YOU'RE *okay now, right?* I asked. *You've totally recovered from the attack at the shifter village?*

Oh yeah, I'm in tiptop shape now. Whatever those shifters did looking after me, it made the cuts heal so fast, I'd hardly believe I got mauled if I hadn't been there. The scars might stick, but that's okay. Just makes me look even more badass.

Well, I'm glad nearly dying didn't put a cramp in your style.

Hey, it'll take more than some murderous werewolves to get me down.

It would. I pictured her beside me, with her perpetual smile and that petite frame topped by her blaring neon-pink pixie cut. A pang of homesickness hit me.

As soon as I can figure out a way to make it work, I'm coming back to visit. Or maybe I can arrange for you to visit me wherever I end up. These "estates" the alphas have are amazing.

Like I said before, if you want to set me up with a quartet of shifter dudes of my own—any time, feel free!

I'll keep that in mind.

She sent a kissy face emoji. *I've got to jet for work. Knock 'em dead at that dinner tonight. Just not literally, obviously, Miss Dragon.*

I tucked the phone away and turned back toward the ocean. So much of my life was up in the air right now, but it was nice imagining some future time when I could just hang out with my bestie in a place like this, no worrying about sudden rogue attacks or fae conspiracies.

The door to the terrace sighed open behind me. Nate's brawny form pushed past it. He was looking even more fine than usual in the formal suit he'd put on, which hugged his muscular body to incredible effect. My breath might have caught a little, taking him in.

His gaze settled on me, and he gave me a smile that looked almost shy. His eyes roved over my body as he walked up to me, but the glint in them was appreciative, not leering. Apparently I was having an effect too.

"That is some dress," he said. "Although it's got to be the woman in it who really makes it."

I smiled back, the compliment warming me. "I like it a lot too. Never been much for dressing up, but I'm starting to think maybe I could get used to it."

"I'd be totally fine with that." He propped himself against the railing next to me, his gaze turning searching. "Aaron told me I'd probably find you out here alone."

My hackles rose, just slightly. "You know you don't have to worry about me being on my own for a few minutes, right? Because I'm completely fine. Just enjoying the view."

Nate held up his hands. "That's not what I meant. I promise. I didn't come looking for you because I was worried. It's..." He ducked his head, the sunlight gleaming off his thick chestnut hair. He was so tall and powerfully built, it still amazed me how gentle he could come across.

"I realized, after what you said the other day when we were fighting off the rogues, that there's something I should probably tell you," he said after a moment, rubbing the back of his neck. "It doesn't *excuse* how I've acted, but I think it'll explain it a little. And... it's an important part of who I am. I'd like you to really know me."

The warmth I'd felt earlier spread through my entire body. I stepped closer, touching his elbow. "I'd like that too. Sorry if I got a bit snappish just now."

"It's fine. I understand why." His smile turned crooked. He took my hand in his, smoothing his thumb over my knuckles. The contact sent a pleasant shiver up my arm.

"You know that the tragedy with your mother and the former alphas happened when we were all pretty young," he said. "I mean, I was the oldest of the four of us, and I was only twelve. And then there was a lot of uncertainty because we didn't know where your mother or you were, or what would happen to our usual way of life..."

"Yeah," I said softly. "That must have been tough. Having all that responsibility and no clear path."

He nodded. "I had good guidance from my advisors.

My kin—we're a little scattered because we're the shifters who don't fit into any of the larger kin groups, but maybe it's because of that we've never been all that competitive. We mostly just want someone leading the way and letting everyone else mind their own business. So I haven't come under exactly the same pressure as the other guys to stay alpha. But I wasn't always sure what I should be doing as alpha either."

"Of course. That makes sense."

"Well... When I was seventeen, and starting to take on more and more of the alpha duties on my own, I got to know another bear shifter whose family worked for the estate. We got along well—she was someone I could just relax with when I had time to myself, someone I could talk to about the decisions I was having to make."

A prickle ran down my back at the "she." My sense of the mate-bond between us twinged. "And then?" I said, managing to keep my voice steady. I'd known not all of the alphas would have waited for me in body as well as in soul. But I wasn't sure I wanted to hear about any earlier diversions either.

Nate hesitated. He had to know how hard it was for me to even think about him with someone else. "For a few years, we weren't anything more than friends. Then after a while, I realized I was falling in love with her. And she admitted she felt the same way. I'd always thought I would wait for the dragon shifter I was meant to be with, but—"

Tears welled in my eyes before the emotion even hit me. I choked on my breath, the thought of Nate—of *my* mate—choosing someone else wrenching through me.

West had mentioned the idea that he might forsake our mate-bond before, but only vaguely. The idea of this specific woman nearly tearing Nate away from me—I hadn't expected it to hit me this hard, but I could barely stand it.

"Ren!" Nate said. He brought his hands to my face, cupping it as he leaned close. I closed my eyes against the tears. "I'm sorry," he said, his voice low and ragged. "I'm *here*. I wouldn't have ever brought it up if I didn't think I had to for us to move forward. I was tempted, and I was unsure, but in the end I chose you. I stopped seeing her— I *haven't* seen her in seven years. I knew that no matter how right things felt with her, being with you would be even more right."

I inhaled sharply, trying to get my reaction under control. "I'm not upset," I managed. "Not on purpose, anyway. I just—the feelings just came over me—"

"It's okay. I can't imagine how I'd feel if *you* talked about wanting to leave us for some other guy." He stroked his hand over my hair and kissed my forehead. I leaned into him, soaking up the heat of his body and the strength of his arms as they came around me.

"The reason I wanted to tell you," he went on, "is to show you that you've always been my first priority. Even when I didn't know you yet, and I had temptation right in front of me. I am so incredibly happy to have finally found you that... I think I've been a little terrified of losing you before we even have the chance to really be together. And I let that fear talk me into being over-protective. I *know* you're strong. I *know* you've got more power in you than any of us. I have to trust in that and not let my worries get in the way."

I hugged him back, nestling my head against his shoulder. "Thank you," I said. "I can see why you'd feel that way. As long as you're *trying* not to act on it..."

"I will. I can't promise that I'll never again give in to the instinct to leap to your defense when you don't really need it—but I'll be doing my best. And if I slip up and you ask me to back off, I'll listen. So don't be shy about telling me off."

A giggle slipped out of me. I swiped away the tears. The wrenching feeling had faded, but an ache remained. An ache for Nate and the years he'd spent alone when he could have had that bond of love already.

I raised my head and touched his cheek. Nate smiled, with so much affection shining in his dark brown eyes that I couldn't doubt for a second he felt he'd made the right choice. I bobbed up on my toes to press a kiss to his mouth.

He kissed me back, softly and then more hungrily. His hand slid down the skin the dress left bare on my back and over the satiny fabric clinging to my hips. A sharper ache settled between my legs. I wouldn't have believed it was possible to want one man this much, let alone four, but I did. God help me, I did.

The murmur of the opening door interrupted those thoughts. The heron shifter I'd seen earlier stepped out onto the terrace, clearing his throat. I stepped back from Nate, not even flushing. After the near-orgy I'd seen in the courtyard yesterday night, it was hard to think a little kissing was going to raise any eyebrows.

"Your presence is requested in the dining hall, Dragon Shifter, Alpha," the young man said with a respectful dip of his head.

"We're on our way," Nate replied. He wrapped his hand around mine and pushed away from the railing. We walked hand-in-hand to the door, not with him leading, but in stride together.

I'd have thought it was a perfect moment if not for the dinner ahead of us, which I knew was going to be anything but fun.

CHAPTER 17

Ren

WHEN I WALKED into the dining hall, at first I couldn't do anything but blink in awe. The room was so big I'd bet you could have fit a football field in there. Long teak tables set for twenty each stood in rows across the hardwood floor. Another of those tables, this one covered with a red silk tablecloth, stood on a dais at one end of the room. Five of the chairs on the far side of that table were carved in an ornate style, with the one in the middle the tallest and most elaborately sculpted.

I didn't need anyone to tell me that was the dragon shifter's chair.

My heart started thudding twice as hard. Other shifters were already moving around the room, talking with each other and greeting newcomers. I felt all those eyes move to me as Nate and I approached the high table. I must have talked to a lot of them last night at the welcome celebration, but somehow this felt different. Then everyone had been partying. Now we were down to more serious business.

Aaron appeared by the high table to meet us. Like Nate, he'd put on a suit for the occasion—a royal blue number that made his eyes look even more brilliant. Damn, I really had lucked out in the mates department, hadn't I?

A woman who looked a few years younger than Aaron, with the same golden-blond hair and bright blue eyes, stood by his side. She studied me with an expression that wasn't exactly unfriendly, but wasn't all that welcoming either. Her dress was a simple Grecian style gown in gray silk, and I could tell from the way she held herself that it wasn't her usual get-up.

Her arms, crossed over her slim chest, were solid muscle. Right. Aaron had said I'd be meeting his sister—the one who'd appointed herself as a sort of bodyguard. She definitely looked the part.

"Serenity," Aaron said, motioning me over. "This is my sister, Alice. Alice, meet Serenity, my mate."

"Hmm," Alice said. She held out her hand for me to shake and squeezed mine tightly as she pumped my arm. "So you're the one who's had my big brother running around all over the country. Glad you finally made it back here."

Her voice was so deadpan I'd have thought she was being snarky, but her lips curled into a playful but warm smile. I relaxed a little inside.

"It was a long trip getting here," I said. "But I did

make sure he returned in one piece, as much as certain rogues might have preferred otherwise."

Her smile grew into a grin. "I'll give you that. And it's probably a good thing he's got someone dragging him out of that library every now and then."

Aaron gave her a baleful look. "The more time I spend outside the library, the more you complain about all the potential danger I'm putting myself in."

"Only when you don't bring me along." She gave him an affectionate pat on the arm and shot me another smile. Okay, I liked this chick.

Aaron escorted me the rest of the way to my special chair, as if I needed help finding it. I guess the formality looked nice for our spectators. And it wasn't like I minded the reassuring squeeze of my shoulder as he took his seat beside me.

I was particularly glad that he and Nate had been the first ones here, because I had them sitting directly next to me on either side. I still wasn't sure what to say to Marco or West. They'd both avoided me all day.

Marco showed up first, sauntering to the chair beside Nate with his usual carefree expression. When our eyes met for a second, his were wary. I dragged my gaze away, my throat tightening. I didn't want to think about our earlier conversation or the revelations it had brought right now.

West arrived a few minutes later. He stalked to his chair without a word or a glance at me and sank into it abruptly.

Alice, who was sitting at his other side, leaned forward to catch my eye and raised her eyebrow. Okay, so that chill wasn't just in my imagination. Was he pissed off because he hadn't meant to make out with me last night? Or was something else going on in that inscrutable wolf shifter head of his?

The chairs across from us began to fill. Aaron introduced me to each figure as they sat down. The Cumberlands, Hubert and Isla. The Porters, Frankford and Tracy. And so on. I caught whiffs of their scent, my instincts and their forms helping me determine their animal side. Hubert and Isla were swans. Frankford and Tracy falcons. The couples around them included hawks, pelicans, and even a couple of geese. I had to bite back my amusement imagining their rounded bellies and long necks in bird form.

"Well," Hubert said to Aaron after a passing nod to me, "I hope the arrival of the dragon shifter means the community can move forward in a more orderly fashion from here on."

Tracy gave a harsh sigh. "It has been a stressful several years."

I'm sure your alpha has been doing his best, I wanted to say, but I bit my tongue. Aaron didn't look offended. And it would probably be a wise idea for me to make a good first impression.

"I've already observed a change in the tone of conversations," Aaron said smoothly. "Seeing the four of us alphas united around Serenity gives everyone the stability we've been needing."

Frankford peered at me over his hooked nose. "And this is the girl we've been waiting for all this time."

He didn't sound impressed. Had he expected me to

come to the table in dragon form? "Here I am," I said, trying not to show how uncomfortable I was.

Servers started to come around with plates of food. Oh, good, at least I'd have something safe to do with my hands—and my mouth. I picked up my fork, jabbed it into a slice of steak... and realized everyone on the other side of the table was staring at me.

My shoulders stiffened. Nate leaned over and said gently by my ear, "At the formal dinners, the tradition is that the five of us don't start until everyone else is eating. It's a symbolic thing, or something."

"Oh." My face flushed hot. I set down my fork as if it had burned me. Great, now I already looked like a nitwit in front of all these bigwigs. The last seven years, mostly living on the streets, waiting to eat often meant someone else snatching your food out from under you. I guessed I was going to need a major attitude adjustment.

"I'm sorry," Aaron murmured. "I should have warned you."

I should have waited and followed their lead. Had West just shot a glower at me? Great, one more reason for him to think I couldn't cut it in this role.

I kept my hands folded in my lap until the servers had finished moving around the room. All around the tables, the estate's guests dug in. When my alphas picked up their silverware, I figured it was safe for me to start too.

Now that I could eat, I had to say the food was freaking delicious. Not that I'd expected anything else after spending a day in this place. I chewed blissfully, letting the rich, tender bites of steak overwhelm my embarrassment.

It wasn't enough to keep Isla occupied, though. She jabbed her fork toward Aaron. "As soon as possible, you need to do something about that feline kin bunch who've been running around in the Southend forestland area."

"I've already started discussing it with their alpha," Aaron said in the same even tone as before. He tipped his head toward Marco, who offered a narrow smile. "It's a big forest. We're all running out of room where we can exercise our animal natures in private. I think we can find a fair division."

I frowned. "Why *divide* it? The cats will mostly be using the ground and the birds the canopy, right? Can't you all use all of it without much hassle?"

Isla pursed her lips with a disgusted expression. Her husband cleared his throat. "There are boundaries in place," he said, shooting Aaron a look as if accusing him of misinforming me. "For good reason. The feline kin have a history of harassing avians. They agreed decades ago they would not intrude on our kin's spaces."

So this was a Sylvester and Tweety sort of conflict? I'd have laughed if it weren't for all those disgruntled looks. I'd put my foot in it again. Shit.

"Oh," I said. "Okay. I didn't realize."

Was that *pity* they were looking at me with now? The back of my neck prickled. Hell, I'd only been preparing for this gig for two weeks, a significant amount of which I'd been busy simply keeping myself and my mates *alive*. Couldn't these people cut a girl a break?

Maybe I should just not talk. That was a surefire way not to sound like a total dumbass.

The talk turned to some event the Cumberlands wanted to organize for the kin group, and then a couple of business concerns I couldn't follow. I cleared my plate, sated but definitely still with room for dessert. Just sitting there, listening to conversation that was going over my head, made me restless. How could I be a proper mate to any of the alphas when every other shifter in the room could see how clueless I was?

Then Frankford started ranting about humans. "We should have bought up that plot of land when we had the chance. Now those people will be right on our doorstep. Making their stupid human assumptions, offering their stupid human advice. So wretchedly unaware."

"But can you imagine the stir if they did know?" Tracy twittered. "The poor creatures couldn't wrap their heads around the power we have."

I couldn't just sit quiet then. "Not all humans are jerks," I said. "My best friend has stuck with me through everything."

Isla gave me another of those pitying looks. "But would she if she found out what you are? I think not."

A flicker of anger shot up inside me. "Well, you'd be wrong. Because she already knows, and she's still got my back."

If I'd thought the shifter bigwigs had looked horrified before, now they looked absolutely aghast. The color drained from Isla's face. Hubert's mouth twisted into a grimace.

"You revealed yourself to a *human?*" Tracy spat out.

Aaron raised his hand for calm. "There were extenuating circumstances," he said. "We made a judgment call. It worked in our favor. Serenity's friend did prove to be a valuable ally."

"To expose not just shifter affairs, but those of our alphas..." Frankford shook his head.

I gritted my teeth. That wasn't enough to contain the rising flare of my frustration.

"Look," I said tartly, "I'm the dragon shifter around here. I'm the only one you've got. If *I* can't make a call about who can know what, who else exactly is qualified to do that?"

Someone down the table muttered something under their breath. Most of it was too low for me to catch, but I heard enough. "...so long away from her own kind..."

My hands clenched under the table. "Does anyone here need a demonstration?" I asked, raising my voice slightly. "To make sure I'm dragon enough for you? I could bring down the ceiling. I could set the whole place up in flames. The shifting part is covered. The rest of the details I'm learning as fast as I can." I eased open my fingers to grasp Aaron's hand, setting it on the table between us. He gripped mine in return, the corner of his mouth twitching up.

"And there's no one I'd rather have by my side while I'm learning than your alpha," I added. "He followed me when I needed his help, and I'll follow him anywhere he needs me to go. Anywhere all of you need us to go, to keep the community strong. So I'd appreciate it if you'd give me a little credit."

Silence hung all around the table for a moment. The

shifters across from us lowered their eyes. Fuck, had I made an embarrassment of myself all over again?

Before I could make any more mistakes, dessert arrived. Perfect portions of strawberry cheesecake for me to drown my sorrows. I kept my mouth shut and watched and listened.

When the meal was over, Aaron stood up, tugging me with him.

"It's an honor to stand before you with my fellow alphas and, of course, my new mate," he said to our audience, pitching his voice to carry through the room. "Thank you all for how welcoming you've been to Serenity. You won't find a more devoted advocate or tenacious fighter for our people."

My face warmed. He said a few more things about how great I was, and I gave a wave to the crowd, but inside I felt unsteady.

The farewells to the guests passed in a blur. Aaron walked me back to my rooms. I let him in and collapsed face-first on my bed with a groan.

"You didn't have to pile on the compliments like that. I'm so sorry for running my mouth. I will never speak again."

Aaron chuckled. "What are you talking about? You *were* great."

I turned my head to raise a skeptical eyebrow at him. "What are *you* talking about? I made a total fool of myself at least five times."

"Not at all." He sat down on the bed beside me, smiling. "You showed them you'd follow our traditions when you knew what those were. That you were willing to take new information into consideration. That you're devoted to the people you care about. And that you've given that loyalty to me. I couldn't have asked for more."

Was he serious? He sounded like he meant it. I couldn't quite believe it, but a little of the tension around my heart fell away.

I pushed myself upright and leaned in to kiss him. Aaron slid his fingers into my hair as he kissed me back. I tried to channel every bit of love and gratitude I was feeling into the meeting of our lips.

My hand rested on his thigh. As I scooted closer to deepen the kiss, my palm slipped. My thumb grazed the hard bulge that had already come to attention in Aaron's dress pants.

Aaron hummed in pleasure, and a different sort of heat washed through me. Suddenly I knew exactly what I wanted to do with this wonderful, gorgeous man.

I trailed kisses along the edge of his jaw as I eased down his fly. When I tugged at his pants, he let me slide them down, watching me with eyes gone heavy-lidded with lust. The sight of it only stoked the fire inside me.

"Stay right there," I murmured, and knelt in front of him.

I flicked my tongue over the head of his cock. Aaron groaned. I grasped the base of his erection, and his hips canted toward me of their own accord. "Serenity," he started, as if to tell me I didn't have to, but I already knew that. I was dying to do it, for me as much as for him.

The man in front of me ruled over a quarter of all the shifter kin with even temper and measured words. But I had the power to make him lose his cool with a simple touch. And there were some parts of him I hadn't fully claimed yet.

I tipped my head, taking his cock into my mouth. The taste of him, even saltier than the ocean air, laced my tongue. I swiveled it around his shaft, loving the way it twitched at the motion. He leaned back on the bed, his hands fisting the covers. His breath was already rough.

I pumped my hand, gradually building speed, as I sucked him down and released him. Over and over, until his body was trembling and his breath coming in hoarse pants. I closed my lips around him even more tightly, and another moan carried into the air.

"Serenity," he said, "I'm going to come. If you keep going..."

Good. That was exactly what I wanted. A tingling grew between my legs as I slicked my lips up and down him. His cock twitched again. His breath stuttered. Then his hips jerked up as his release hit the back of my mouth.

"Serenity," he muttered. "Serenity." His hand stroked over my head. And just for that moment, nothing else mattered—not betrayals or lies or scheming rogues and fae. There wasn't a single thing in the world that could hold me down.

CHAPTER 18

Marco

IT WAS hard to say what the most terrible moment in my life had been, but it had definitely happened in the last twenty-four hours. Maybe at the top of the list I'd put hearing the pain and anger in my princess's voice when she'd accused me of treating her like a cat toy yesterday. Maybe these few seconds now, knocking on the door to her rooms at eight in the morning and wondering if she'll even answer.

Soft footsteps padded over the rugs on the other side. My back tensed. Ren eased open the door.

No, this was the most terrible moment right here. Having to watch my Princess of Flames flinch at the sight of me, the wound I'd dealt her still blazing clear in her eyes. It cut me from heart to gut with a sharp, searing burn that I absolutely deserved.

Why the fuck hadn't I kept my mouth shut for once

in my life? Why had I let those idiot kin of mine rile me up?

Why had I let myself start thinking about my mate like a means to an end, even a little? I knew *she* deserved better. I could give her better. If she ever gave me another chance.

But I wasn't going to grovel and moan. The pain I was feeling was my own fault and mine to deal with. I'd be twice as much an ass if I tried to lay that on her too, as if she should comfort me through my epic screw-up.

"Princess," I said with a dip of my head. "May I come in?"

She hesitated, and that just about killed me. Less than a week ago I'd tasted her most intimate places, and now she wasn't sure she even wanted me in the same room. It was going to be a long, hard climb back.

But she was worth it. I just had to make her believe I believed that.

I forced a self-deprecating smile. "I can make my apologies here in the hall if you'd rather. But I promise I'm not planning on imposing for very long."

"No," she said. "All right. Come in."

She must already have been up for a while. I could smell the traces of soap mingling with the sweet scent of her freshly washed skin. She'd picked out another dress: dusty rose-pink silk, simpler than the one she'd worn to the formal dinner last night but no less regal. It clung to her slim curves in a way that provoked a flash of desire all through my body.

She hadn't chosen it for breakfast with her mates,

though, I'd guess. That was her armor for meeting the fae monarch.

"You'll put her fairy highness to shame," I said, nodding to the dress.

Ren brushed her hands over the flowing fabric, looking briefly awkward. Then she drew her posture straighter again. "I just want her to know she's dealing with a different kind of monarch," she said. "What was it you wanted to talk about?"

As if she couldn't guess. It was hard to hold her gaze while I pulled together the words, but I didn't want her to think I was shying away from responsibility. "Like I said, I need to apologize," I said. "You're right to be angry with me. I should never have talked about you that way, to anyone. I can't tell you how much I wish I hadn't. And I hate even more that you had to hear it."

"So why *did* you say those things?" she asked, crossing her arms over her chest.

God, how to say it. The words tasted bitter as I formed them. "There's a certain... air of confidence I've found I need to show when talking to my kin. Especially the ones who might have an eye on my position as alpha. If they think nothing much affects me, they don't find any weaknesses to exploit. But I shouldn't have let that extend to you. I owe you so much more respect than that."

Ren's eyes studied me steadily, giving away nothing. "Do you owe me it?" she said. "So you're telling me nothing you said to your kin reflected your real feelings, even a little?"

I couldn't lie faced with her dragon shifter

sensibilities. She'd know, and that would only dig me deeper into this hole.

"I meant what I told you in the caves, princess," I said. "I care about you. I want to spend my life with you. But I can't pretend I'm not also aware that my position will be more secure once our bond is consummated. I may have pushed too much. I'm even more sorry for that."

There was so much more I could have said to try to explain, but I could read her too. And with the avian upper class sniping at her and this fae parlay looming, she clearly was in no mood for excuses.

The excuses were beneath me anyway. I'd screwed up. I owned that. What really mattered now wasn't what had happened in the past, but what I did from here on.

"I understand it'll take time to get your trust back," I added. "But I will, however long it takes. I may talk a lot, but I don't give my word lightly. I promise you I'll earn that trust back honestly."

Ren nodded. I couldn't tell whether she accepted the promise or just wanted me out of her sight. "Thank you for the apology," she said carefully. "I guess we'll just have to see how it goes. I'll need some space, so I can think."

Of course. When we were close to each other, our mate-bond still pulled her toward me as much as me to her. I could be grateful for that much.

I dipped my head. "Until our field trip into the fairy realm, then."

She didn't say another word as she saw me out. The

door clicked shut behind me, and I couldn't say my heart felt any less heavy.

Ren

My head was so full of questions and worries about the upcoming parlay that I barely had room in there to decide how I felt about Marco's apology. I hardly had room to even pay attention to where I was going.

I followed the smell of eggs and sausage down the hall to the private dining room. My stomach was tight with anxiety, but I was going to need energy for this meeting with the fae monarch. I had no doubt about that.

How was she going to react when I told her what I know her people had done? How was *I* going to react if she tried to brush it aside or deny it? Aaron's people would be *really* unimpressed if I managed to bring the shifters to the brink of a supernatural war less than a month after I'd shown up to take my spot as dragon shifter.

A woman came out of the dining room and headed toward me. I distantly registered her scent (owl), the tray she was holding (must have been bringing or clearing food), and the thin gloves covering her hands (was it colder than usual today?). Then my mind went back to mulling over the day ahead of me.

I wasn't paying her any attention at all when she dropped the tray at my feet and rammed a carving knife toward my stomach.

My shifter reflexes kicked in before I'd even processed that I was under attack. I leapt to the side, smacking out with my arm at the same moment. The knife only nicked my belly.

The woman gave a little cry and threw herself at me. I grabbed her wrist before she could take another slash. Scales rippled over my body as I started to shift defensively. I loomed over her, my haunches growing, my claws extending, fire rippling in my throat.

"Ren!" Nate's voice carried from behind me.

Another distraction was *not* what I needed right now. "Stay back," I shouted, my voice gone hoarse with the partial transformation. "I'm handling this."

The woman squirmed in my grasp. She aimed a kick at my hip, but it glanced off the thickly scaled skin that had formed there. She jabbed at my eyes with her free hand. I jerked away, and my grip on her wrist loosened. She broke free and took another stab at me.

With a growl, I knocked her to the floor. The knife sliced across my shoulder. I swiped at it with a taloned hand, sending it flying into the wall. The woman stared up at me, her eyes wide with what now looked like panic. I pinned both her arms to the floor, staring at her as I caught my breath.

The gloves suddenly made sense. She had to be hiding her lack of a kin mark.

I had her trapped. I'd stopped her, and now she couldn't get away. We could finally talk to one of these rogues—whatever good that might do us.

Nate's footsteps sounded behind me. He'd hung back like I'd asked him to. I shot him a quick, fierce smile over my shoulder. "Thank you. What do you say we find out what she knows?"

"You've got this," he said, coming to stand beside me. "Let me know if you need me."

But now that I had the rogue, I wasn't sure what to say. "Why did you attack me?" I asked, fixing my stare on her again. "Are you on your own, or are there other rogues here?"

"I'm not going to tell you anything," she gasped out, and set her lips in a firm line.

"Are you part of the group that came after my mother before—that murdered my fathers and sisters? How did you even get into the estate?"

She looked back at me without a word. Frustration boiled up inside me. The heat collected in my throat, and my mind leapt back to the words I'd heard as I'd accepted the crystal's flame in the mountain.

Burn away lies to get at what is real.

The urge to breathe fire tickled in the back of my mouth. I could do it—I could shift all the way, spill my fiery breath over this woman. But I'd never tried to use this new power before. What if I used it wrong, and all I did was burn her alive?

I'd hurt people while fighting them in self-defense before, but this rogue was already subdued. And being set on fire—that wasn't defense, that was torture. Every bone in my body balked at the thought.

That wasn't how I wanted to start my reign over the shifters. The rogues were the cruel ones, not me.

"Serenity?" Aaron had come out of the dining room.

He stiffened at the scene in the hall. The rasp in his voice thickened. "What happened?"

"She attacked me with a knife—looks like one from the kitchens," I said. "But she's refusing to talk."

How did you make someone talk if you *didn't* resort to torture? I peered into her eyes, trying to find an answer there. She blinked, and a strange impression came over me.

The way she was gazing up at me... it wasn't angry. It wasn't even entirely afraid anymore.

She was in awe of me. I felt it, like a rush of warm air. And under it, a tight knot of sorrow. The pieces clicked together in my head.

"You didn't really want to do this, did you?" I said, letting my voice soften.

The woman's jaw twitched. A shadow of that sadness crossed her face. I'd hit the mark.

The door at the far end of the hall murmured open, but I didn't look back to see who was joining us. All my awareness stayed focused on the rogue.

"They forced you to help them," I said gently. "Did they threaten you? Or someone you care about?"

Her composure broke. A little sob fell from her lips. Her eyes had filled with tears.

Aaron knelt down at my other side. "I swear you will not be punished for crimes you were coerced into. By my oath as alpha." He held up his hand with the oath scar etched in the palm. A pulse of power tingled over me.

The rogue must have felt it too. A few of her tears spilled down the sides of her face. "They have my son.

167

He's only seventeen. He's all I have. If they find out I told you..."

"They won't," Aaron said firmly.

"And we'll stop them. We'll get your son back." I glanced at Aaron, and he nodded his approval. "Where are the rogues who took him?"

"I don't know," the owl shifter said in a thin voice. "Everything is passed through messages. I never see them face-to-face."

"Are they planning anything else? Do they have anyone else working for them on the estate?"

She shook her head. "I don't know. They only told me that if I managed to— If I—" She couldn't seem to spit out the words.

"If you killed me," I prompted.

"Yes. Then they'd return my son. That's all I know."

I bit my lip. I wanted to help her. I wanted to take down every one of the rogues who'd forced someone like her to take the fall for their schemes. But we couldn't when this was all she knew.

"We'll do what we can for you," I said, "but we'll need you to help us too. Find out more about them, where they are, what else they're doing. Who's involved. Anything, so that we can track them down. We won't reveal that we caught you. You can pretend you're still waiting for your chance, but that you want to do more for them. Act like you've decided you agree with them so they'll trust you. Can you do that?"

"If it gets my son back, I'll do anything." She dragged in a breath. "Thank you for your mercy."

I pushed off her, watching her as I stood. She sat up,

no sudden movements, no sign she meant to try another attack. She might have bruises on her wrists from my grip tomorrow, but I couldn't help that. From the expression on her face, she wouldn't blame me for them.

"I'll make arrangements for you to get word to me, wherever I am, when you have any news," Aaron said.

"And of course we'll be keeping our own eyes out for your not-kin," West said in a brittle voice. Marco stood just behind him. Some relaxing breakfast this was turning out to be.

Aaron helped the owl shifter to her feet and ushered her off to the side to talk with her further. I sighed, leaning my hand against the wall.

The rush of adrenaline was fading, leaving me shaky. The lovely dress I'd picked out in the hopes of impressing the fae monarch at least a little was now torn around my legs from my partial shift. The skin on my belly stung where the carving knife had pricked it. The cut on my shoulder was only seeping a little blood now, but it still ached.

Nate slid his arm around my shoulders. "Let's go back to your rooms and patch you up." He shot a glance at his fellow alphas. "Have one of the servers bring a plate for her."

West glowered as if he resented the order, but Marco accepted it with a quick nod. "Not a problem." He looked toward the rogue woman, and his lips curled into a grimace. "And might I suggest you keep the door locked until the food gets there?"

CHAPTER 19

Ren

BY THE TIME Nate and I made it to my rooms, my legs were done. I wobbled over to the sofa in the sitting room and sank onto it.

Nate ducked into the bathroom. He came back with a small silver case that turned out to hold pretty normal-looking first aid supplies.

I winced as he dabbed antiseptic cream on my cuts. He smoothed a thin adhesive bandage onto my shoulder and considered my stomach.

"I guess I should take this off," I said, reaching for the straps of the torn dress. "Being a shifter does seem to be hard on one's clothing supply."

Nate chuckled. "We always make sure to have lots of spares on hand."

I stripped the silky fabric from my body, leaving me in only my bra and panties. It was impossible not to see the heat kindling in Nate's gaze as he watched. An answering dampness formed between my legs. I swallowed hard and held out my hand for the other bandage.

He stood back while I attached it. I still didn't feel ready to stand up. I held out my hand to him, and he sat down beside me, collecting me against him—my bare legs across his lap, his arm around my shoulders, loosely so I had room to move away if I wanted to.

What I wanted was closer. I nestled against his solid body, letting the warm and strength in it soothe me. I didn't know the question was coming until it fell out of my mouth.

"Are they ever going to stop? The rogues—are they ever going to just leave me alone? I never did *anything* to them... They don't even know me!"

"I know," Nate said in his low baritone. He tucked his chin over my head and rubbed the side of my arm. "I don't even understand what they did sixteen years ago. To carry around that much hate, to want to hurt people that much... They're sick. Their minds are twisted. That's the only thing I can think."

"Then they won't stop. They'll just keep at it until they kill me—or we kill all of them."

"Maybe they'll be able to change their minds once they do get to know you." He pressed a kiss to my forehead. "You're already becoming a part of our community. Most of the kin are welcoming you—you've seen that, haven't you?"

My mind went to the iciness of the bigwigs last night, but the truth was they were just a small portion of the shifters, even if they were powerful. Most of the kin I'd met—the avians here, the canines in that other village—had thought more of me than I even did.

"Yeah," I said. "They've been wonderful, actually. I'm not sure I deserve it yet."

"Of course you do. By fighting back against the rogues, which you've done more than once already, you're fighting for all of us. For the security of all kin. And what you did just now, with that owl shifter... You proved you're trying to do the right thing for all shifters, even the rogues. People will see that. Word will be passed on. And the ones who aren't so twisted might realize they're wrong."

I wasn't sure whether I believed that was likely, but it was a nice thought all the same.

A knock sounded on the door. I couldn't help wincing. Nate gave my arm a reassuring squeeze and went up to answer it. He came back with a plate of breakfast foods that set my stomach grumbling.

For a few minutes, my hunger shoved our conversation to the wayside. I dug into the scrambled eggs, sausage, and hash browns as if I hadn't eaten in days. Shifting sure gave a person an appetite. Or maybe it was the adrenaline. Either way, I polished off the food like my life depended on it.

"Better?" Nate asked with an amused smile.

"Much." I set the plate aside and snuggled closer to him, wrapping my arm around his brawny chest. We still had a couple hours before we needed to leave for the parlay. And being with him, holding him and being held by him, was the best salve I could think of for my nerves right now.

What had the shifter who'd delivered my breakfast thought of this situation—of my hiding away in my room? That question brought my thoughts back to Nate's earlier comments.

"No one here really knows me yet," I had to point out. "Not even the people who like me. They're still waiting to see exactly what I'm going to do."

Nate hummed in agreement. "Maybe, but they're hoping it'll be good. They want to be on your side."

That was true, wasn't it? I'd felt that hope in every shifter I'd spoken to during the celebration. And with each step forward, I could give them a little more to justify their faith in me.

It wasn't just the ordinary shifters who had faith. My alphas had stood by me from the start, from when I'd been a total stranger to them, too. No matter how skeptical they might have been.

And Nate hadn't wavered once. He might have gotten over-enthusiastic with the heroics, but he'd never talked to me or acted in any other way like he doubted me.

I tipped my face back and touched his cheek. Nate didn't need me to tell him what I was looking for now. He bent his head, capturing my lips with a soft but eager kiss. His hands skimmed over my body, grazing every inch of bare skin. I slid my hand up under his shirt as I kissed him harder, wanting to feel him too. To explore every plane of that firmly muscled chest.

To really make him mine.

The thought swam up in my head through the haze of longing. No hesitation rose to counter it. The idea just felt *right*.

I tugged at Nate's shirt. He peeled it right off and leaned in for another kiss. Every spot his bare skin touched mine left me burning with even more desire. He stroked his hand up my back and worked the clasp of my bra free. As he trailed his kisses down to my collarbone, he cupped my breast with his strong, able fingers. His thumb swiveled over my nipple, sending a jolt of pleasure through me. I moaned, arching up on his lap.

He tipped my breast up to his mouth and teased the nipple even tighter with his tongue. My fingers dug into his shoulders. Pleasure coursed from my chest down to my core as he laved one breast and then the other. His hand followed his mouth, flicking and caressing until both nipples stood at stiff peaks and the rest of me was trembling.

"I love seeing how good I can make you feel," Nate murmured, nuzzling the side of my neck. "I love that I can take care of you this way. I've never wanted *anyone* like this, Ren. My heart always knew you were the one I needed."

A pang hit me, bittersweet. He'd taken such a chance, waiting for me. Giving up the happiness that had been right in front of him without ever knowing if I'd turn up.

I slid my hand around his neck and pulled him into a deeper kiss. My other hand rested on his lap beside my legs. On the hard length of his erection straining against his fly.

Nate groaned into my mouth. He eased his fingers up

and down my hips, teasing the edge of my panties. Asking but not demanding. My tongue slipped into his mouth to tangle with his. For a long moment, I rode on the rush of pleasure that came from our mingling breaths. Then I pushed myself off his lap, pulling him with me. Toward the bed.

"I need you too," I said.

Nate gazed at me with a sudden intensity. He got up and stepped over to me, looming above me from his full height. But it was a reassuring loom. It made me feel larger that a man like this wanted me this much, not smaller. I hooked my fingers over the hem of his pants. His breath caught.

"Ren," he said, wonderingly. He touched the side of my face, so much tenderness in that powerful hand.

"I want you to be my mate," I said, gazing back at him. "And I want to be yours. From now until always."

"Hell, yes," he said. He bent to crush his lips against mine again. I gripped his shoulders as he walked us back toward the bed. When my legs hit the foot of the frame, I reached for the button of his pants. He kicked them off, and his boxers too.

For a second I just gazed at the perfection of his body. Six-foot-something of solid muscle and soft skin, all for my taking. And his cock, thick and long and standing at attention for me. Growing even harder when I stroked it from base to head.

Nate rumbled low in his chest. He scooped me up and laid me on the massive bed, making quick work of my panties. But the impulse to take control came over me. I nudged him onto his back and knelt over him. He grinned up at me, resting his hands on my hips.

"Lead the way. I'll be right there with you."

A rush of affection flooded me. I lowered my lips to his, kissing him long and hard. But too much desire had built up between my legs for me to wait long. I rubbed my sex against his cock. We both moaned. Inhaling slowly, I lowered myself right onto him.

His cock filled me completely with a heady burn. I whimpered, rocking against him until he was all the way in. He reached up to fondle my breasts with one hand while the other stroked over my clit. The combined sensations set off a flood of bliss that swept every other thought from my head.

I rode him desperately, chasing my release. He pumped his hips up to meet me. His breath turned ragged. A sheen of sweat dampened his muscled chest as I braced my hands against it.

"I want to watch you come," he murmured, swirling his thumb over my clit. "Take everything you need, sweetheart."

Something about those words sent me over the edge. The glow of our bond flared between us. It flowed over me, surrounding me in the protection I knew Nate would always offer me, whenever I needed him.

I bucked against him a few more times, and pleasure burst through my body. I gasped, clutching him. He caressed me through the wave, his eyes bright with appreciation—and a deeper desire.

Even as my nerves sang out, I wanted more too. Harder, faster. I sagged against him and gave him a little tug to roll us over. He flipped us without slipping out of me. I raised my legs on either side of his hips to give him even deeper access.

"More," I said. "Take me higher."

He thrust inside me with a shudder. "You feel so good, Ren. So fucking good."

A moan broke from my lips. "So do you. Give me everything. I can take it. I want it. Don't you dare hold back."

With a sound halfway between a groan and a chuckle, he thrust faster. Our skin slid together, slick with sweat. Every muscle in his body felt coiled beneath my groping hands, driving his shaft into me with everything he had. Just the way I needed it.

The pleasure swelled and swelled until I was shaking with it. I arched up, taking him all the way to the hilt, and another orgasm swept through me. Nate jerked with a hot gush inside me. His head bowed over me as he rocked to a stop.

We lay there, panting, for a long moment. I traced my fingers over his cheek, and he beamed down at me, so brightly it sent a flutter through my chest.

"I don't know how I got so lucky," he said, "but I'm sure as hell going to make sure I deserve it."

"Mmm," I said, pulling him down to cuddle against me. "I think this was an *excellent* start."

I fit against his body perfectly. His heart thudded beneath my ear where it pressed against his hot skin. I pressed a kiss to it, wishing I could stay here like this for the rest of the day.

His fingers glided up and down my back. "We'll have to get you back into another dress soon."

"I know. But not yet." Five more minutes without thinking about the fae monarch and what she might have in store for us—that was all I asked.

I nestled my head against his shoulder, closing my eyes against the rest of the world and the worries that came with it.

CHAPTER 20

Ren

Insects hummed around us as we tramped along the narrow path through the woods. The mossy smell in the air was kind of pleasant, but the terrain? Not so much. I glowered at a jutting root I'd nearly stubbed my toe on.

So much for getting a break from hiking after that long trek up and down the mountain. We'd driven most of the way to the neutral ground that lay between the avian estate and the fae monarch's domain, but apparently the fae found any sort of man-made transportation distasteful. Arriving to meet them with a motorized vehicle would have been a grave insult. So we were walking.

Which, frankly, was a grave insult to my feet, but I wasn't in a position to make demands on that big a scale yet.

It'd have been easier if I could have at least *flown*, but

I was still pretty much a newbie when it came to shifting. The last thing I wanted was to blow my wad of energy before we even got to this fairy queen. From everything I'd heard, I was going to need all my wits and power for that confrontation.

My alphas had stayed in human form—so they could talk to the monarch too, I guessed, and probably also to keep me company. But a few of Aaron's kin had joined us as their bird selves. Alice had squeezed my hand and told me to give the fae hell before taking off as an eagle nearly as large as her brother's. A shrike, a raven, and an albatross were soaring over the forest alongside us as well, watching for any suspicious fae activity.

Aaron strode along in the lead, scanning the forest with his watchful eyes. Marco sauntered after him with his feline grace. West was walking as far behind me as he could manage without running into Nate, who was guarding our flanks.

The bond between me and my eagle and bear glowed through me with a comforting heat. But I was just as aware of my other two mates and the nagging pull toward them, begging to be fulfilled. Especially West. Even though he was keeping his distance, my back kept tingling with the sense of his gaze on me. A sudden, more heady kind of heat: there, then jerked away, then there again.

I tugged at the skirt of my new dress to lift it out of the way of my shoes as we scrambled up a small rocky slope. This one was a crimson silk instead of the earlier pink, but I liked it too. It was a color that said I wasn't one to take any nonsense.

Which I wasn't, with fae or with my mates.

I slowed my pace until West had no choice but to let me fall back beside him. The path was just wide enough for us to walk side-by-side, though I had to make a conscious effort not to let my arm brush his. He looked straight ahead, his jaw tightening.

"Is this really how we're going to do this from now on?" I asked. "With you going around all day acting like I've gravely offended you somehow?"

"None of my responsibilities as alpha demand that I pander to you," he retorted.

"Oh, please. In the last two days you've been friendlier to the furniture than you've been to me. I'm not saying you've got to throw me a party. I just don't see why you've got to completely freeze me out."

I heard him swallow. "I think you know what the problem is, Sparks."

A flare of anger I hadn't expected shot through me. Because I didn't know. Because nothing about how he was acting seemed remotely reasonable to me.

I raised my chin. "I can think of a whole lot of things you might be pissed off about, but I honestly haven't got a clue why you seem to be pissed off at *me*. You want to be my mate and you also don't. Fine. Take all the time you want figuring that out. When have I ever said anything else? I'm not trying to push you into anything. The most I've ever asked you for is a kiss, two weeks ago. So be frustrated with yourself, or the situation, or, hell, even my mom for how she handled things. But I don't see how it's fair for you to take that out on me."

Silence hung between us for a minute. There was

nothing but the rasp of our feet over the uneven ground. I started to wonder if I'd pissed him off even more. Then West inhaled sharply. His voice came out even throatier than usual.

"You're right. I haven't been completely fair. I'm sorry for that."

Some of the tension in me ebbed. "So... we can move to at least polite conversation?"

The corner of his mouth twitched. "Maybe some. That's not really my forte at the best of times. Don't push your luck."

He hadn't said much, but the space between us felt less fraught now. I was about to pick up my pace and give him the breathing room he obviously wanted when he added, "So I guess we're heading to the bear shifter's estate next."

There was an odd note in his voice that squeezed my heart even though I couldn't say exactly why. "What makes you say that?"

One of his eyebrows lifted. "The five of us are all bound together to some extent, Sparks. When you confirm that connection with one, you'd better believe the rest of us know it."

My cheeks warmed at the thought of the other guys sensing what Nate and I had been up to a couple hours ago.

But why shouldn't they know? Eventually, the way things were meant to be, it *would* be all of us.

I rubbed my mouth. "Ah. Well, yeah, I guess it would make sense to visit Nate's kin next. The way things are."

West made a noncommittal sound. I wasn't sure what

to make of that. But the conversation seemed to be over, so I sped up. We had to be getting close to the meeting spot anyway. I couldn't afford to be distracted from that.

The path had swerved. Aaron was just disappearing from sight up ahead. I hurried even more, my nerves prickling—and a bright feathered shape swooped out of the sky in front of me.

Alice transformed as she plummeted, but with complete control. She landed on her feet with a thump, her hands already rising in a defensive stance. She'd kept her eagle talons protruding from her bare feet. They looked nearly as sharp as my dragon claws.

Before I could take another step, Alice's right arm shot out to motion me back. I halted. My ears perked, but I didn't hear anything ominous in the forest around us. "What's wrong?"

"That tree." She waved a fist at the broad juniper a few feet ahead of us by the end of the path. "Something's off about it. It got this... glint to it when you came close."

The tree? I cocked my head at it, but it still looked like a totally ordinary plant to me. Alice took a few steps closer, totally at ease in her nakedness. I'd been around shifters enough in the last few weeks that their casual nudity was starting to seem a lot less weird to me.

The muscles running through Alice's sturdy frame tensed. The guys had stopped, Aaron backtracking. "What's going on?" he said.

"I think there's a trap in this tree," Alice said, jabbing a taloned foot toward it. "But Serenity is the one it's set to activate for."

Marco sniffed the air. "There is a whiff of fae around

here. I assumed it was from their arriving at the meeting place."

"It sounds like there's an easy way to find out," I said. "Why don't we see what the tree does if I come closer? Unless you don't think it's worth the risk." Alice clearly had a lot more experience in this kind of situation than I did.

Her mouth flattened, but she nodded. "Slowly. And be ready to retreat."

I edged one careful step and then another along the path. Nothing moved in or around the tree. Maybe she'd been wrong? I trusted her instincts, but we were also all a little on edge.

I eased my foot a few more inches forward—and all at once the entire tree lunged. Its trunk wrenched forward and its branches dove down as if to swallow me in their grasp.

I ducked, stumbling backward. Alice leapt to meet the tree. Her leg slashed through the air, talons severing one branch. Her elbow slammed into another to snap it. A shower of leaves rained down on me. I spun back toward it, a shift already prickling under my skin.

Alice stood panting, her lips curled in a fierce grin. Twigs and broken branches scattered the path. The battered tree had pulled back into its original pose as if it had never moved.

"What the hell was that?" I said.

"Alice was right," Aaron said. "There must be an enchantment on the tree. It was set to descend on you when you came by. As soon as you backed away, the effect lifted."

"A *fae* enchantment," West spat out. "What else could use magic like that?"

My heart thudded. "Do you think—the monarch—"

"She wouldn't *dare*," Nate rumbled in a low, dark voice. A grizzly's rage flashed in his eyes.

"She wouldn't," Marco agreed. "But we've already seen that her underlings don't mind finding ways to circumvent the treaties. A few bad apples, I'm sure she'd say."

West bared his teeth. "It doesn't matter. We take responsibility for the rogues. Every fae is hers to deal with."

"And we'll make sure she does," Aaron says. "When we meet her. It's almost time." He glanced at me. "If you give the tree a wide enough berth, the trap shouldn't activate again."

I nodded. With one last glare at the juniper, I picked my way through the brush on the other side of the path. The tree didn't stir. I let out my breath when I'd come around the bend, back onto the somewhat clearer ground.

"I'd better get back to the skies in case they've got more surprises for us," Alice said. Her legs flexed to spring into the air.

"Thank you," I said quickly, catching her gaze. "I've never seen anyone fight a tree before, but you were pretty amazing at it."

Her grin came back. "Nothing's ever gotten the better of me yet. I'll have your back, Serenity."

I appreciated the promise, but I approached the neutral meeting spot with my nerves even more on edge. I was finding it less and less easy to believe that the fae monarch was an ignorant bystander in all this. Whatever friendship there might have been between fae and dragon shifters before, something had gone very, very wrong.

The trees thinned and then fell away completely. We came out into a wide clearing, nothing but grass and a dabbling of little pink flowers from one end to the other. The sky was stark blue overhead. The warm breeze warbled faintly through the branches around us.

We'd only taken a few steps into the clearing when the fae delegation appeared on the other side. There had to be at least ten of the tall, emaciated-looking figures with their blue-white skin. The cloying smell of them made my nose wrinkle.

At the front of their procession strode a woman even taller than the others. The silvery blond waves of her hair streamed across her shoulders and down over her filmy dress all the way to her ankles. Her large eyes glittered like black diamonds. A faint shimmer rose off her hair and skin. A crown of living vine coiled around the top of her head, but even without that, I'd have known she was the monarch.

My back stiffened, but I kept my expression as calm as I could manage. We walked to meet the fae in the center of the clearing, Aaron and Nate drawing close by my sides, West and Marco flanking us. The other avian shifters circled in the air just overhead.

"Monarch," Aaron said, with a slight dip of his head. "We appreciate you coming out to speak with us."

The fae woman's gaze barely glanced off him. She looked me over, her face impassive. "So this is the new dragon shifter."

So this is the woman who killed the last one, I wanted to say, but I held my tongue. Direct accusations of murder weren't very diplomatic. "Here I am. It's good to meet you." *So I can finally get some answers.*

"And what is the reason for this parlay?" the monarch asked, her gaze sliding back to Aaron now. As if he were more worthy of her attention than me.

I couldn't help bristling a little. "*I* requested it," I said, "because I have questions about the fae presence in the mountain over Sunridge. And also, now that I'm here, about the enchantment placed on a certain tree along our path through the neutral ground."

The monarch frowned, her eyes carefully blank. "Sunridge? The name sounds vaguely familiar, but I can't say it's a place I've given much consideration. And I know nothing about any tree."

Yeah right, she didn't. "There was magic on it," I said. "An enchantment for it to attack me. No one except a fae could have done that."

"Are you sure? You haven't exactly had much exposure to our kind, have you? From what I understand, you haven't seen much even of your own people."

Okay, now my hackles were *really* up. Was that how she wanted to play this? Nate stirred, but I held out a hand for him to stand down. I didn't need him fighting this battle. I wasn't going to make it far as dragon shifter unless the fae monarch learned to respect *me*.

"I know enough," I said. "And I have my alphas when I need extra guidance. I didn't need any help at all to see what your people did to my mother on that mountain."

A flicker of something passed through the fae

woman's face, so fast an ordinary human wouldn't have caught it. But I wasn't human.

"The last I heard of your mother, she'd run off from the kin groups many years ago," the monarch said, but she was lying. I felt it through every bone in my body.

I drew myself taller. Maybe not as tall as her, but I had a whole lot more meat on my bones, so I had to look a little intimidating. "There is a treaty between your people and mine. You will take responsibility for the crimes committed by yours. But if you really want to try me, go right ahead and lie to my face again."

Behind me, Marco smothered something that might have been a snicker. A chill glittered in the monarch's eyes. "*Are* these your people?" she said in a cutting voice. "From what I can see, you've barely accepted two of their leaders as your chosen mates. And you're speaking to me of responsibilities?"

My throat went abruptly hot, fire flickering at its base. My skin tingled with the itch to take on its scales. I kept the impulse to shift in control, just barely. "It's still my life. I will make my choices in my own time. I'd have been more ready for them if your people hadn't taken my mother from me. But I *am* ready to make you answer for those crimes."

Aaron took a slight step forward. His voice rang out. "As alpha of the avian kin, I stand with Serenity Drake completely."

Nate lifted his head. "As alpha of the disparate kin, I stand with Serenity Drake completely."

Marco moved to stand at Aaron's side. "As alpha of

the feline kin, I stand with Serenity Drake completely. And I will for the rest of her life, wherever it takes her."

I'd never heard him sound so serious. A piece of the hurt I'd still been feeling fell away.

Before I could wonder if the wolf shifter would extend his loyalty that far, he appeared next to Nate. "As alpha of the canine kin, I stand with Serenity Drake completely. When she demands your respect, she speaks for *all* of us." He glowered at the monarch.

The fae woman made a faint sniffing sound. "I have told you what I know. I have seen no proof of the crimes you claim. If all you've called me here for is baseless accusations, I've given you enough of my time."

She swiveled on her heel. Her fae attendants parted around her to give her room to pass through.

She really was going to just walk away from me. As if I had no authority at all. As if she owed me *nothing*, after everything her people had taken from me.

No. She was going to learn right this moment what a mistake it was to dismiss this dragon shifter. It didn't matter how long I'd been gone or how some of the bigwigs might talk about me. I was here now with my alphas by my side, and I claimed this power as mine.

"Stay right there," I snapped, my voice already hoarsening. I had just enough wherewithal in my fury to tug off my silk dress as the shift came over me.

My muscles stretched and sang, the burn only pleasant now. Flames seared the back of my lengthening throat. I rose and loomed, flexing my massive wings.

The fae monarch whirled around. She didn't look so tall now, standing beneath my dragon's body. I peered at her with narrowed eyes. She gave me a cold smile. A crackle of magical energy glittered around her body.

"To attempt to harm me would be an act of war," she sneered.

But I didn't want to harm her. No, the sizzling in my throat was the fire of the crystal, the fire of that gift of truth. I'd been afraid to try to claim it before, but I shouldn't have been. It *was* mine, and I trusted myself. This woman needed to know exactly who she was dealing with.

I opened my mouth and breathed from deep down in my chest, where a ring of loss ached around my heart.

Flames poured down over the monarch. They shattered her protective shield. Her attendants shrieked. But the flames weren't the bright yellow and orange fire that would have burned her to a crisp. They flickered white and violet, surrounding the fae woman in sharp shards of light.

Burning through to the truth.

Her eyes widened. Her lips parted, her hands clutching at the base of her throat as if she were trying to hold back her voice. But it spilled out anyway, wavering through the flames.

"I heard of your mother's death," she said, sounding choked. "I knew a group of fae were responsible, but no one else did, so I let it be. I have not punished them. There are others I've heard speaking out against the shifters. I haven't encouraged them, but I haven't stopped them either. If one used magic against you today, I can easily guess who it was."

Her attendants fell back around her, gaping at her

admission. Aaron fixed her with a stare of steel. "Why have you let those crimes slide?"

The monarch's lips twisted, but my flames still surrounded her. "It's been easier for us while the shifter community was disordered. We've been able to claim more territory, refuse more compromises. I was happy to let that situation continue."

I winced inside at the admission. A hotter fire tickled the base of my throat, wanting to punish *her* for all the hurt she'd allowed to happen. I held it at bay and sent another gust of the truthful flames over her. My dragon form was starting to quiver with the strain of this unfamiliar power.

"Will you accept Serenity's authority and ours from now on?" Nate asked.

"Yes," the fae woman gasped. "As much as I have to."

I didn't like the sound of that. But I couldn't produce another burst of flames. I let them peter out, just barely holding on to my dragon shape. I stayed there and glowered down at her.

The monarch rubbed her hands over her arms as if trying to dispel the fire that had already vanished. She stared up at me. For the first time, I saw fear in her eyes. Fear—and a hint of rage underneath it.

I'd gotten the better of her this time, but she wasn't going to forget it. Whatever conflict had been brewing between the fae and the shifters, it was far from done.

"These accusations don't seem so 'baseless' now that you've admitted they're true, monarch," Marco said archly. "Where do you say we go from here?"

She seemed to catch a scowl. "I will make

reparations," she said. "The fae who have acted against the shifters in any way will be punished according to the treaty. So will others in future if I hear of it myself. You have my word."

That last sentence settled in the air with a supernatural finality. We could trust her at least that far. I guessed we couldn't exactly ask her to commit to *feeling* any particular way about the shifters.

I bowed my head, blinking at her, and a shiver passed through her skinny body. "Does that resolve our business here?" she asked.

"Other than one thing," Aaron said. "When you address your people who've acted against us, that should also include any who've helped rogue shifters make attacks on us or the rest of our community. Agreed?"

She nodded with a jerk. "Agreed."

She shot me one last look before she turned with a sweep of that flowing hair. A look that told me she was beaten for now, but not forever.

But as victories went? I'd take that.

When the fae had disappeared back into the forest, I released my dragon form. My body crumpled with a shudder. I gasped a breath down my suddenly sore throat. The power I'd been granted had felt amazing, but it'd left my body throbbing.

Nate offered me my dress. I slid it back on, regaining my balance. "All right," I said. "Let's go home."

CHAPTER 21

Nate

"I DON'T KNOW why I feel so shaken up," Ren said. "I already knew she was dead, and that the fae killed her."

She rubbed her hand over her face. We were standing in her bedroom in front of the mirror where she'd been combing the dark brown waves of her hair. They spilled smoothly over her shoulders and the neckline of the teal dress she'd chosen for tonight's farewell gala. Tomorrow we were moving on to my estate to the south.

I rested my hand on the small of her back, and she leaned into me automatically. Touching her had always made my heart leap, but nothing could compare to the steady heat of the connection that now thrummed between us. A bond that should last as long as we both lived.

"You didn't know how much approval those fae had from their monarch," I said. "You had to hear her talk as if your mother's murder meant nothing to her. Of course that bothered you."

"Yeah. I guess that makes sense." She drew in a long breath and squared her shoulders. "Back out into the fray."

I chuckled, taking her hand as we headed for the door. "Just remember that you did what you came here to do. We can't bring your mother back, but we are getting justice for her. And you got it using the power she always wanted you to have."

Ren nodded, her hand rising to the hollow of her throat.

The courtyard in front of the avian estate was already teaming with shifters, like it had been when we'd first shown up two nights ago. A band was playing a jaunty tune on the steps, and people everywhere were dancing. Ren swayed my arm in time with the music, but I had two left feet when it came to keeping a rhythm.

"I think I'd better hand you off to Aaron if you're in the mood for dancing," I said with a grin. The eagle shifter was already making his way over to us.

"I'll be back," Ren said, with a quick peck on my lips. I watched as Aaron swept her away, spinning her and dipping her. Our dragon shifter laughed, her eyes shining, and the warmth in my heart grew.

She was finding her home here with us, in spite of all the tragedy in her life before now.

"And we're staking our livelihoods on *that*," a voice muttered just behind me.

The grizzly in me bristled automatically. I glanced around and spotted one of the couples who'd been sitting across from Ren at last night's dinner—one of the ones who'd sniped at her for every minor mistake. The man was the one who'd spoken. The woman was shaking her head in dismay.

"I know. It's shameful."

I gritted my teeth against a roar. My fingers itched to sprout my claws and smack those two bird-brain heads together. My hands clenched—and then I remembered everything Ren had said to me before.

She wouldn't want me making a scene in the middle of this party on her behalf. I could defend her without going into full bear mode.

"You'd almost think—" the husband started, and I cleared my throat, turning all the way toward them.

"You'd almost think what?" I said, letting my voice drop just low enough to be mildly menacing.

The couple startled, their stances stiffening. The man's jaw tightened. "I'm allowed to have whatever opinions I happen to hold about the people ruling over us."

"True," I said. "But if you'd seen how Serenity brought the monarch of all the fae to her knees earlier today, I don't think you'd be complaining. Or do you think *you* could make the fae tremble at the sight of you?"

His mouth opened and then closed again as he struggled for words. Yeah, that's what I'd thought.

"Talk to the guards who came along with us if you don't trust your own alpha's word," I said. "They'll tell you just how powerful our dragon shifter is."

"I suppose we will," the woman said. She grasped her husband's elbow and tugged him away. Which was for the best, because if they'd tried to take another jab at Ren, I couldn't have promised I'd have kept my animal instincts in check any longer.

"Defending our dragon shifter's honor again?" West said dryly. He'd come up beside me while I'd been distracted.

I frowned at the wolf shifter. "If you're here to snark, I don't really want to hear it. After this afternoon, even *you* have to admit she's something special."

West's gaze slid past me to where Ren was still dancing with Aaron. Her hair flew out around her face as he whirled her around. Joy and love shone on her face. I couldn't figure how any of us could have seen that and not felt his heart melt.

And maybe none of us could. West's expression softened slightly. So did his voice. "Maybe I do," he said. "Watching the monarch turn tail and flee... That really was something, wasn't it?"

A glow of pride filled my chest. "That was our dragon shifter."

That was my mate.

Ren

A sudden hush fell over the crowd around Aaron and me. We'd just stopped to catch our breaths after dancing for three songs straight. I looked up, and my body tensed.

A thin, pale figure had appeared at the edge of the courtyard, gleaming against the darkness. A fae man. He held his hand up with a motion I instinctively knew was a truce gesture. He meant no harm here.

But that didn't make me happy to see him.

Aaron stepped forward to meet the fae man, and I followed. The man's searching gaze stilled when it landed on us. He held out his other hand, which was shining with a sharper light.

"The monarch wishes you to know her word has been kept," he said. He whipped his hand upward.

A scattering of tiny lights burst apart over our heads. The fragments glittered and faded into the cooling night air.

"What—" I started, but the fae man had already vanished. Murmurs rose up through the crowd, startled and awed. I turned to Aaron. "What was that all about?"

He looked up at the sky where the lights had disappeared, his expression solemn. "The monarch followed the terms of the treaty, according to their laws. The fae who acted to harm us and your mother have had their lights snuffed out."

"Oh." My stomach balled. I followed his gaze, thinking of those lives wiped out.

Just like they'd destroyed my mother's life. Just like they'd treated the rogue the fae woman in the mountain had claimed they'd found stalking us. That was how the fae worked, apparently. Quick and brutal.

Not the kind of enemies I really wanted to keep.

"The conflict between us and them isn't over, is it?" I said.

Aaron's mouth set in a grim line. "No, I don't think it is. But we're better prepared for whatever they try next than we've ever been before. And now my kin have all seen the sway you hold over them too."

He looked at me and smiled. I couldn't help smiling back. Maybe it was okay to pretend, just for a little while, that all our problems were solved.

The celebration wound down as night thickened around us. My eyelids were heavy by the time I found myself meandering down the estate's hall toward my rooms with my four alphas in tow.

When I caught sight of my door up ahead, a longing squeezed tight around my heart. Some part of my mind tripped back seven years to the nights curled up in the otherwise-empty apartment that had been my mother's, waiting with less and less hope every time to hear her key in the door.

I never wanted to feel that alone again. I shouldn't, now that I'd found my mates. But just knowing they'd be on the other side of those walls suddenly didn't feel like enough.

Nate moved to head to his own rooms, and I held out my hand. "No. Stay with me?" My gaze slid over my other mates: Aaron calm and steady, Marco amused but slightly uncertain, West as gruff as ever. "All of you. I want you to stay. Please? I'm not asking anything more than that. I just don't want to sleep alone."

I knew Aaron and Nate didn't really need to be asked. Marco gave me his sly smile and said, "As you wish, Princess of Flames." West looked as if he'd bit back a scowl, but he inclined his head, as if to say he'd go along with the request begrudgingly.

Apparently he decided he needed to actually say it

too. I held the door while they all filed in, and he paused in front of me. "Look, Sparks, what I said in front of the fae monarch doesn't mean—"

I rolled my eyes. "Of course," I said. "No commitments assumed. Now come on. I'm exhausted —aren't you?"

I climbed into the middle of the massive bed and settled amid the spread of pillows. The guys surrounded me, Nate and Aaron cuddling right up to me on either side. Marco and West kept a little more distance, but I hadn't expected anything else. I could still feel our bond winding warm and solid around me. The five of us altogether, the way I knew down to my soul it was meant to be.

My nerves settled. My body relaxed into the bed. I drifted off into sleep, encased in the certainty that no matter what troubles lay ahead, I was exactly where I belonged.

A frantic knocking shook me awake. I blinked in the dark room as my mates stirred around me. With a huff of breath I recognized as West's, one of the guys pushed off the bed and stalked to the door. The rest of us sat up. I rubbed my bleary eyes, my heart hammering.

"What is it?" West muttered as he opened the door.

A quavering voice carried through the sitting room to the bed. "We've just gotten word. There's been an attack on the bear alpha's estate."

ABOUT THE AUTHOR

Eva Chase lives in Canada with her family. She loves stories both swoony and supernatural, and strong women and the men who appreciate them. Along with the Dragon Shifter's Mates series, she is the author of the Demons of Fame Romance series and the Legends Reborn trilogy.

Connect with Eva online:

www.evachase.com
eva@evachase.com